Atomic City Crime Story

Ray, Hope you enjoy it

Ray Nelson

*to Jean and Andrew for your support
and to Steve and Marcie,
fellow atomic citizens.*

This is a work of fiction. Names, characters and places are invented or used fictitiously. The events depicted are imaginary although the role of Hanford Patrol in protecting the safety and security of the Hanford site during the cold war stands on its own. What authenticity this story has comes from listening, as a small boy, to men talk.

Chapter One

Nate was on a toot. As Bill pulled into the gravel parking lot of the Starlite tavern; Nate was bent over talking to a guy in an old tan Ford. Nate had one hand on top of the car, the other holding a can of Hamm's, waving it around, telling the guy some kind of story. Suds dripped off the can onto the back window of the car. The guy in the Ford raised his hand and pointed at Nate, who backed up a step.

Bill angled into a parking spot nearby. His 1940 Harvester pickup rumbled and quit. Nate turned his head fast. He slapped the top of the Ford twice, putting a period on his sentence, drained his Hamm's and walked over to Bill's truck. The Ford pulled slowly out of the lot. As it drove off, Nate raised his hand, half wave, half get lost motion. Even half in the bag, he moved with a sly grace for a big man; a testament to his 23 knockouts as a light heavyweight in the service.

"Crimony Slim, you look like a dirt farmer in that beat up heap," Nate said, smiling. He poked his head into the open window of Bill's rig, eyes slightly out of focus. Nate smelled of beer, onions and too much Aqua Velva.

Bill opened his door, sliding Nate back a foot or two. "Nice to see you, too." He stepped out on to the gravel lot. The night was warm after the blazing hot August day. Bill pulled the front of his shirt away from his chest.

"Hell, Slim," Nate said, "Just bustin' your chops." Nate reached behind Bill and slammed the door shut. "Let's go get a beer." They took a few steps, Nate kicking gravel as they walked. "Hey Slim, we okay for Wednesday?" he put his fingers to his lips whispering. "No need to mention it to Aggie, mums the word." Nate strode off to the door of the Starlite.

Bill took half a step and stopped, "Aggie's here? Jesus H. Christ Nate, we could have gone to someplace nicer, instead of this skull and eyeball joint."

Nate was up the steps next to the Hamm's sign, blue and yellow neon tubing framed by the window next to the door. "That's why you're here, Slim," Nate said. "She wouldn't of come if it was just me." He pushed his way through the door to the large smoky room. "Besides Captain, we got to celebrate your promotion."

Bill took the two steps, shouldered next to Nate. "Hold up a sec," the smells of the bar mixed with the desert wind and the willow smell off the river. "What's up with the guy in the Ford?

"Just some wise ass," Nate said, squinting his eyes narrow in the smoke.

Bob Wills and the Texas Playboys were playing on the juke box. Out in the back courtyard Bill could see the band setting up. The retractable roof of the Starlite's dance floor was open, to the half-light the moon made above. Aggie Bourbeau, Nate's sister, had been sitting at a table near the bar. As they came in she stood up.

"Let's go out back, it's cooler," Aggie said. She turned and without waiting for the two men walked out to a table near the dance floor, under that evening sky. Bill and Nate followed, her Mexican print dress swishing past the edge of the bandstand.

Seated at the small table, Nate spread his arms, "My two favorite people, Sis and Slim," he rat-a-tat-tatted on the table top. "Gotta have drinks, I'm buying." He pointed his finger like a pistol and then walked off to the bar, snapping his fingers to strains of The Yellow Rose of Texas. He turned his head grinning at them, "I know what you two like."

Bill pulled a pack of Camels out of his shirt pocket and offered one to Aggie. She shook her head and he lit his own with his Zippo. "Good to see you again," he said sucking his cheeks just hollow enough to get the Camel going, "When was the last time, June?"

"Uh-uh," she smiled, "Try, March. Purex reception." She looked at him and Bill saw the resemblance to Nate. Same dark features, dark eyes, sharp nose, long legs. It looked good on her. "I'm surprised you remembered at all," she said.

Bill held his cigarette away to keep it out of her face "Course I remember," he said. "You were hard to miss. All those Poindexters and you," he pointed at her with his cigarette hand, "And they let you cut the ribbon." Bill gave it a smile.

She crossed her legs, rearranging the yellow and crimson print of her dress. "You looked pretty serious, in your uniform, like you might shoot someone if they clapped too loud," she said, as she reached for his pack of cigarettes and shook one out. She had long tan fingers, nails cut short with no polish.

He lit her cigarette, her hand almost touching the back of his trying to steady the flame.

"I'm only allowed to wing 'em if they clap too much," he said.

She turned her head and blew smoke away from the table. "Say, I need to ask you," she said. "You know, Nate..."

Who then reappeared with his big hands wrapped around two beers and a tumbler of something icy. Nate sat down with the drinks. The band, a five piece dance combo launched into a Tommy Dorsey tune, it was *Blue Tango*. Nate took a long pull draining a good third of his beer and began tapping his feet. It was getting too loud to talk. That was OK with Bill; he had exhausted his small talk.

"Come on Sis, let's dance," Nate said, as he pulled Aggie to her feet. The band had juiced up the swing number and a few couples were on the dance floor. Nate and Aggie outclassed them all. Nate had one arm around Aggie and pulled her into a spin. He smiled as she matched his steps. The other couples were a mixed lot; young construction and trades workers, taking their wives and girlfriends out, a Hanford Process Operator still finding his way around town, all newly arrived to the desert.

Bill parked his cigarette in the ash tray. He held the straw colored liquid up to the light trying not to be too interested in the backside of Aggie's dress. The song over they sat, Aggie fanning herself. Nate leaned forward, his black hair plastered on his forehead, "That was a good one, Sis. Thanks for staying off my new shoes."

She punched him hard on the arm, "What are you talking about, Bobo, I taught you how to dance."

Nate held up his hands like a boxer hiding his face. "Sure, sure, sure. Thought maybe you forgot how, working with all those eggheads."

She turned to Bill, smiling for the first time that night, "See what I have to put up with?"

Nate was looking around the bar, "Your turn Slim, I think Aggie needs a new dance partner."

The band had started a slow tune, *I'm Yours*, and before Bill could say anything, Aggie stood up, "Come on," she held out her hand, "I won't bite. Too hard."

Bill didn't know whether to set his beer down or drain it. Normally a smooth character, he pushed his chair back holding on to the table, not wanting to stumble. They moved to the dance floor, green painted concrete. The desert sky was just fading to black, the moon brighter. He held her as they moved, hoping she didn't notice his hands were sweating. She was tall, in her heels they looked eye to eye. Her eyes were brown with flecks of gold.

"Don't worry, I won't break," she said, as she shifted a bit closer to him. She smelled of soap and sun.

"Yeah but I might." Maybe she wouldn't notice his gimp knee. "I've never danced with a physicist before."

"I've never danced with a cop," she said. "Brothers don't count. Most physicists don't know how to dance."

"Most physicists don't look good in a dress either," he said, smiling over her shoulder. Looking up he could see the wind had come up. A branch of an old locust tree could be seen above the roof line swaying, casting shadows on the dancers.

The drummer worked his magic with his brush and high hat, the saxophone held a long low note at the end. At the end of the dance, Bill could see she was distracted. As they stood apart from each other the gold flecks in her eyes changed. As they walked to the table," Bill," she said, "You know, Nate, I worry about my little brother."

The chair where Nate had been gulping his beer was empty. The mug was sweating on the table top, two inches of foam in the bottom.

"Where is he? He's been searching for someone all night. I thought it was you, but maybe not." She shrugged her shoulders and took a long drink on her Tom Collins.

"He'll be back in a minute." Bill looked around, hoping to spot him, decided to change the subject. "Did Nate help you get on here?"

She laughed, "Not a chance. I was here from the start, well a few months out at Los Alamos, but then I came up here just as they finished construction on the first pile, in '44. How about you?"

Bill gazed over her shoulder and the swaying locust branch, the desert wind bringing tiny amounts of sand that glittered in the lights of the band stand. "I was born here." He said.

She glanced up from Nate's empty glass, "Huh?"

"Born here. Grew up just across from the White Bluffs. We had orchards and cattle." Bill stopped. This was the place where people got that blank look. Aggie, on the other hand, looked interested.

"You mean the little towns that were here before they built Richland."

"Rebuilt it. The government village incorporated the old town site. You know the brick shell north of the 300 Area?"

"Yeah, I always wondered what that was." she said.

He said, "That's where I went to high school." Bill pushed Nate's beer mug in little circles leaving a wet trail on the table.

"So what was it like?" She said.

Bill pushed Nate's empty mug away from him, "What?"

"Here, before the war." Aggie placed both her hands around the still cold mug.

"Different. Dead quiet. Just a couple of little farm towns." He lit another cigarette.

Aggie peered down into Nate's mug. "Were you in the war?"

"Why do you ask?" He sat back, knocking ash into the tray.

"You got the look, like Nate, plus you're about the right age." She waived a hand.

"So what about you?" Bill finished his beer.

"Nate and I grew up in Montana, outside Bozeman. A busted ranch. I got a scholarship to Montana State. Majored in physics" She said, "and learned to dance."

"I went to Pullman." Bill said.

"What was your major?"

"Drinking, mostly." Bill raised his hand, signaled to the waitress for another round.

"Where in god's name is he?" Aggie started to get up.

Bill made a sit down motion with his hand, "Let me go see."

Bill got up and walked toward the front door. Stopped by the Hamm's sign, *From the land of sky blue waters,* spelled out in yellow neon illuminating the front lot. Bill could see the Ford again, this time with two men in it. Nate was talking to the man on the passenger side, who handed him an envelope. He turned and strode toward the door stuffing the envelope into the back of his pants. Bill walked back to the table.

Nate came back in, sat, fingers drumming the table. "Hey sis, did I tell you Slim here got promoted? Yep, he is now a Watch Commander."

Aggie took it in, then turned to Bill, "Congratulations, what does that mean?"

"You mean more than an extra 20 bucks a month?" he said. The waitress put three more drinks down, took the empties.

"Sure" she said

"Not whole lot. The Patrol has commanders for each shift. I get to fill out extra paperwork, sign the logs and transfer all the badge requests. What's your clearance anyway?" Bill moved his chair sideways, crossed his legs.

"Q, but you probably already know that." she said

"You are high up there."

Aggie stood and said, "Bill, you owe me one more dance." She waggled her fingers at him.

Bill stood, grateful that it was another slow one. He could swing, but nowhere as graceful as Aggie or Nate for that matter. His hand on the small of her back, he could feel the taut muscles on either side of her spine.

"This is better." she said.

"Hmm?"

"You've loosened up."

The song ended too soon. Nate was sitting at the table, nursing his beer. As they walked up Aggie announced, "Time to go little brother. I have to be in fabrication by eight."

"Aw come on, I'm on long change and back on nights. Sit and have another drink." He signaled the waitress.

"Nope." Aggie said. Bill could see them squaring off. Aggie stood next to the table, picked up her purse.

"One more," Nate said smiling, "I'm flush for once."

"Nope. See you later." She turned to Bill, "Walk me out to my car, OK?" She turned and headed for the door.

Nate bowed his head into his beer. "Sure, go on; leave me here by my lonesome."

Aggie rolled her eyes and faced Bill squarely, "Ready to go?"

Out in the parking lot, the smoke and the noise of the bar behind them, the quiet of the night settled in. Aggie walked to a late model Chevy.

Bill said, "Hey, is this yours?"

She opened the door and settled into the cream colored driver's seat, "You sound surprised." the car started with a deep purr.

She pushed her hair back behind her ear, "Thanks for the dance, Bill. I am worried about Nate, maybe you can find out what he's up to." She drove off, out of the lot, toward Richland.

Back inside. Nate was talking to the waitress, who seemed to like the attention. The band had taken a break and the juke box was on loud. Bill sat and sipped the last of his beer. The waitress came over, stopped by and put a hand on Nate's shoulder. Nate made to order another round.

"I have to go, bud. I start early." Bill said. "Do you have a car?"

Nate looked up at the waitress, winked. She giggled. "Naw, Aggie's the only one with wheels; mine got busted up awhile back."

Bill stood, "Let's get you home."

"Aw come on, have one for the road. I told you I'm flush." Nate gestured to the waitress.

Bill shook his head, "You coming or not?"

Nate looked at him, "Not. Don't worry, I'll get a ride."

Chapter Two

Bill woke before 6:00, his usual time in the long summer days. The light slanted through the house, promising heat. He made coffee and silently thanked Aggie for getting him away from Nate and the Starlite. He had too much to do today. On his first day as a new Watch Commander he wanted to be sharp. He stood by the sink, looked out the window, across the desert to Rattlesnake Mountain; down the long brown slope of the treeless sage covered ridge that shown in the morning light. The desert steppe fell down to the Yakima River. His property started on this side of the river, ten acres of sagebrush and sand, with the little house at the end of the road. Across that river, to the top of Rattlesnake and beyond, down to where the Columbia made its grand sweep south and all of 450 square miles was the Hanford Works Project. Born in the depths of World War II, it was a critical link in the Manhattan Project that ended it in the firestorms of Hiroshima and Nagasaki.

This was the new history of this area. A history that started in 1942 when the government came in and claimed all of this part of Washington State for the war effort. It was an area that had three things that the War Department needed for the Manhattan Project: a ready source of power from the newly completed Grand Coulee dam, abundant water for the cooling of the plutonium production reactors being built, and isolation to maintain the biggest secret of World War II. This south east corner of Washington, close to the borders of Oregon and Idaho provided all three. The government came in, and with the expediency of the war effort brought in 50,000 workers, set them up in trailers and barracks, and put them to work. Only a very few knew what they were doing, the rest were told it was necessary to end the war. In August of 1945 the Richland Village newspaper ran the headline answering everyone's question: "It's a Bomb!"

He walked out of the house carrying his hat and gun belt and put them in his truck. His grey Hanford Patrol uniform was crisp, but the black stripe of his trousers would be wilted by the end of the day. He started down the gravel road next to the Yakima River heading toward the West Richland Bridge. He had an easy drive across the bridge and up the Yakima River floodplain, across the railroad tracks and into the government built town. The summer sun was in his face as he drove through the streets of government built houses; 'A' houses, 'B' houses, 'F' houses, precuts and prefabs to the center of the city. The Army Corps of Engineers built the town and it had all the charm of a municipal water plant.

Right in the center of the town was the 1100 Area, a fenced and guarded two square blocks that held the administrative buildings for the Hanford Works Project. As the new Watch Commander, Bill's day would be filled with the government's business, keeping the government's secrets. Mostly this meant doing the job he had been doing unofficially for the last month, filling out traffic reports, scheduling rotations of officers and the endless security checks necessary for this huge project. As usual, at 11:30 he took his lunch bucket with a thermos of too sweet coffee and two baloney sandwiches and walked east to the little park by the river. Here, if he squinted, he could almost imagine the Richland of his youth, a dusty small farm town by the rolling Columbia. The trees towered over the park and their interlocking branches formed a cool island of shade from the summer sun.

After lunch Bill returned to the 1100 Area downtown. Two sets of fences, a guard station and a drop gate kept unauthorized people out. Inside were a series of brown and tan single and double story buildings. They could have been on any military base or government project anywhere in the country. They had all the government issue markings as did every other building in town. Bill parked in the sandy lot in front of the FBI offices. It wasn't marked except as building D-4. Like many things at Hanford and Richland, if people wanted you to know you were told. Nondescript as it was, this FBI office was the largest on the West Coast.

Agent Parker was at his desk and looked up when Bill came in. He was young and eager, but Bill generally thought he was less of a dick than the other agents. He was also more permanent. Agents rotated in from Portland and Seattle. There were at least 15 agents at any one time. A few were permanently stationed here and Parker was one of them.

"Agent Parker," Bill said as he handed him the stack of personnel files he had retrieved from his office.

Agent Parker, looking cool in his summer weight, striped gray flannel suit took the files and signed for them. Anyone who applied for work at Hanford went through a background check. Their personnel files went from the personnel office to the FBI, then to the Hanford Patrol for badge assignment. More personnel were being hired right now. Bill knew they were increasing production at K reactor pile. Something big was on, but he wasn't paid to be curious.

"Thanks Bill, got a sec? It's about the Franklin case." He pushed out a chair. Bill took off his hat and sat down. He was curious what Parker was going to say. "We traced the last pieces and everything is tied up." Everybody knew about the Franklin case.

Parker went on summarizing, as if he were in court, "Jerry Franklin, a carpenter's assistant in the 300 Area, drives by newly dug ditch half filled with fifty-five gallon drums. From the road he could see one filled with equipment and tools. They looked unused, and he helps himself. He gets out of the truck and fills his carpenter's long box with tools thinking he has just made a great find. On the way out the Patrol checks his roster and sees he is checked out to the 1100 area downtown. The guard looks and sees his carpenter's box but not the tools underneath. Jerry hides the tools in his home. Two weeks later a monitoring van starts squealing as it drives by Jerry's house, the Geiger counter is off the setting.

"So how did all those tools get crapped up in the first place?" Bill had heard several versions of this story.

Parker hesitated. Bill as a watch commander had a Q clearance. Still, Parker was technically violating procedure by saying anything. Bill liked that about him.

"A cask was being loaded for a trip." Bill knew he meant that finished plutonium was being readied for a trip to Los Alamos. "They had been working in Purex and left the tools out." He went on, "Product was sorted for shipment next to the tool case by mistake. Doesn't take long."

Pilfering went on all the time at the plant. The Patrol kept an eye on it. Bill knew his officers sometimes looked the other way. They kept a handle on it but this had been a big screw-up, one he was at least partly responsible for.

"What about Taggers?" Parker had retrieved a file from a cabinet.

"Officer Taggers was reprimanded and a formal letter was placed." Bill leaned forward, "We switched him to the Vernita Barricade for a month."

The Vernita Barricade, located at the extreme northwest section of the sprawling complex was considered Siberia. There was very little traffic, and you were stuck in a six by six guard house staring at an empty road. Routine calls on the radio and spot checks kept you awake.

"Unless the Bureau is considering other charges." Bill let the comment hang.

The uneasy relationship between the FBI and the Hanford Patrol had taken years to find a balance. The Patrol was a creation of DuPont and G.E. after the war when they took over control of the Hanford Engineering Works from the army. They guarded the gates, patrolled the perimeter, checked the physical security of the buildings, and acted as law enforcement on all areas of the project. In 1950 they were sworn in as Benton County Sheriff's deputies. This cleared up any legal issues and increased their ability to serve warrants and make arrests. Another division of the Patrol made up the Richland Village Police. The town was not incorporated and all the land and buildings were owned by the federal government.

The Bureau treated them like they were amateurs. Bill and many of the older men, especially the vets, respected the FBI but thought most of the agents were out of touch with the realities of the project. The FBI agents were mostly city boys, well educated, and well intentioned, but after they had gone through the J. Edgar Hoover charm school what little common sense they had, left.

Parker was different. He had grown up in Spokane, went to college at Gonzaga and joined the Bureau in '44. As one of the permanent agents he lived in town and had a family. Better than all of that, he actually listened to you when you spoke.

"We feel sure you can handle it." Parker said. He stood and closed the file.

Bill took this as his cue to leave. Back out in the sun, the desert heat enveloped him. It was 4:30 and shift change. The bright flat light made his eyes hurt. On Jadwin Avenue, the gray Hanford buses lurched toward the south neighborhoods. Men in khaki pants or dungarees, sport shirts rolled up, got off with their lunch pails. He stepped into the motor pool building, checked in his patrol car, and signed out for the day. Back in the lot he crossed to his own vehicle. He removed his gun belt, took off his hat and placed them on the bench seat. He took off his jacket, folded it neatly and laid it on top of the hat and gun. He started up the truck and headed for the gate. He slowed at the gate and flashed his badge.

Riley, the guard made a note on a clipboard. "Slim, when you gonna get a new car?"

"Probably when you get a new hairpiece." Riley unconsciously touched the toupee that stuck out under his patrol cap.

Bill drove north on Wilson, all the windows open, the dry hot air sucking the moisture off his skin. He had grown up with this summer heat. By August each year his skin had turned a dusky red brown. You learned what everyone does in the desert, work like hell from before sun-up until noon, stop in the middle of the day and get in the shade, then resume again in the long summer twilight. But that was before. Now it was three shifts: days, swing and graveyard. There were regulations for working outside, regulations for working indoors. Everything was by the numbers, and safety first.

Bill remembered another heat, a different heat from the Pacific War. Bloody Buna, a little speck on a map that men from the Northwest were sent in to take from the Japanese Imperial Army. The light was almost like today, flat and angled, the sky almost white with the tropical heat.

The Higgins boats dropped their ramps. Bill and his company struggled through the knee deep water to the beach. The Japanese troops were dropping mortar rounds into the water but not doing real damage. Beyond the dirty brown beach the jungle came down almost to the shore. To the left cliffs rose steeply and were lost in the haze. The dampness and heat stuck to you so you thought you could not take a breath. After weeks of bloody fighting, they were taken off the island. One in four of Bill's men were dead or wounded.

Bill got through without a scratch. He was promoted and made a captain. It was on return from Buna, on the troopship on the way to Australia that the letter from his father had caught up with him, saying that he had sold the ranch, his holdings, and had moved to Prosser. Thunderstruck, Bill could not imagine why his father had done that. His inheritance, all that he had worked for, was gone. His father had only said, "You will understand when you get home."

He had of course, but it was a long time coming. It was not until after V-J day. When Bill was serving occupation duty in

Japan he put it all together. His father had been forced to sell everything to the government at rock bottom prices for "the war effort". No one knew anything other than that the whole area from Priest's Rapids to the Yakima River was taken over by the Army. The towns of Richland, Hanford and White Bluffs were bought wholesale along with all the farms and ranches in the surrounding areas. More than once, however, as Bill drove through the shattered, burned and bombed out sections of Tokyo he had thought, "It could have been worse."

He had stayed in the Army for an additional three years in Japan, working with the Provost's office. He had come to respect and admire the Japanese people as they slowly put their lives together after the war, struggling back from unimaginable loss and destruction. Bill, like many veterans of the Pacific War, had no qualms about the use of the atomic bombs. After the fighting in Manila, they had begun preparing for the invasion of the Japanese home islands. None of them thought the Japanese would ever give up. They all knew in their bones that they would die. The atomic bombings and the Japanese surrender came as a complete surprise, and for many, their lives started again. Everybody had heard the rumors and read the accounts of what went on in Okinawa.

The next morning Bill was on his way to inspect the 100 and 200 Areas. Each area was filled with production reactors taking enriched uranium and creating tiny amounts of plutonium, or processing plants for chemically separating the uranium from the plutonium or both. They had their own shifts of guards. Each area was separated by miles of desert. As a Watch Commander it was his responsibility to make monthly inspections. The long drive up from Hanford Patrol headquarters to the reactors and plutonium processing plants along the Columbia River would take him past the old White Bluffs town site. Aggie had shown more than a passing interest in the little towns and ranches that were pushed aside and abandoned to make room for Hanford. The whole Hanford Works were built in the place of White Buffs and several other small farm towns along a twenty mile stretch of the river. In their place now stood the jumbled gray concrete blocks of the production reactors, turning tons of enriched uranium into ounces of plutonium.

Bill had the windows down in the grey Hanford Patrol car. He felt the dry and still cool air of the desert and could just smell the moist air off the river. Why was Aggie worried about Nate? He knew Nate could be shady but thought underneath it all he was a straight guy. He was a force of nature, a good friend who would do anything for you if you caught him in the right mood. A friend, but the kind of friend who was a lot of work.

The police radio under the dash swelled with static. He reached over, turned up the volume and squelch. He couldn't make out the dispatchers voice. He picked up the hand mike and pressed the send button. "Say again?" He said, "Over."

Nothing but static, but he thought he heard a voice trying to break through. He fumbled with the hand set as he passed a brick building gutted of windows, most of the roof missing, willows and scrub locusts grew around its foundation. "Say again," he said. "Over."

Back from the foundation the football field had been reclaimed by sagebrush. He slowed to the shoulder next to the field and thought of his high school graduation in 1938. The desert wind bent the dry locust branches. He worked the radio changing channels, trying to draw the voice in. Through the windshield high voltage lines towered over the rusted goal posts, channeling electricity to and from the reactors.

"Christ on a crutch." he muttered at the windshield. "No wonder it won't work."

He stomped on the accelerator, speeding away from the goal posts, the power lines and White Bluffs of 1938.

The radio crackled, the voice clear, "Code 20. Robie called in a code 20."

He pushed the hand set button, "Say again. Over."

"This is an all call for Commander Bill Rosen. Code 20. 100kw officer Robie Gardener called in a code 20."

"This is Officer Rosen. I read you loud and clear. Code 20. Please report location."

"Reported location is 100kw. Over"

"Location is 100kw. Over."

He sped up. Sagebrush, a jackrabbit, tumbleweeds, tumbleweeds and power lines. The squad car high revving into a throaty howl meadowlarks and crows, made it in less than 15 minutes.

The 100kw reactor, all gray concrete walls and sharp angles jutted up from the river's edge telescoping 200 feet into the air. Power lines snaked to and from the central power stack. Officer Robie Gardener, tall, thin and looking grim stood next to the open door of his squad car. Bill stopped on the dirt service road, the wind kicking dust toward the bend in the river. Gardener bent down to Rosen's open passenger window. "We got a body," Gardener said. "It's one of ours."

Without another word Robie got into Rosen's patrol car and pointed him around the west corner of the reactor loading bay.

"How did you find out?" Bill said. "Who is it?"

The service road circled around the front of the building to the huge pipes that would open, dumping tons of hot radioactive water into the cooling ponds.

"I was in the gatehouse out front." Robie said. "That technician, that boy Price, called me."

"What was he doing?"

"He had just suited up to do the run check." Robie checked his watch, "He just came on an hour ago."

Rosen had patrolled this reactor and its several acres of ponds for the last four years. He knew every yard of the sandy berms, the count of the graphite control rods, the number of security lights, the depth and color of the water. He knew what it should look like. In four years he had written 200 reports describing this scene. He stopped the patrol car, got out and walked to the top of the berm.

Today was different. It would be a different report. What was different was at the north end of the active pond toward the river, a body floated face down. It was wearing the unmistakable uniform of the Hanford Patrol, gray shirt soaked black, dark wool pants of one leg pushed up to show an inch of white leg above black boots.

The technician, Price, in white coveralls and white cloth head covering came toward them. He wore gloves and a respirator mask dangled around his neck. In his hand he had a Geiger counter. From twenty yards Price shouted and waved his arm.

"I wouldn't get any closer," Price said. "It's gonna be six hours, at least."

Price got right next to the two patrolmen and held his arms out cautioning them. "Look, we had a hot run last night. Gotta stay back from this for now."

Rosen started along the top of the berm, ignoring the technician, to get closer to the body. Officer Gardener held his ground not knowing if he should follow Rosen or stay back.

Price raised his voice. "Didn't you hear me? We had a hot run, the body's gonna be coming out hot."

Rosen snapped a little mock salute, waving him off, "Okay, you said what you had to say. I got a body and a job to do."

"Look I'm warning you."

"I know you're doing your job, fella, but I've been out here for years." Rosen pointed to the north end of the pond and the river beyond. "I know how close I can get and how long I can stay. I need to size this up and see if we got a crime site or a mule deer."

"Just hold on there officer," he said for the record. "I need to get a supervisor out here."

"You do what you need to do." Bill turned and shouted to Robie. "Get a rope out of the squad car; we got to get this cordoned off before we have technicians and supervisors crawling all over this place."

"I still gotta call my supervisor." Price shouted as he turned and walked as fast as he could in his bulky coveralls down the short slope and back to the monitoring shack between the pond and the reactor cooling tower.

"Follow him, Robie," Bill said. "Let him call whoever he wants. Don't forget the rope." Bill started toward the body then shouted back at Robie. "Is the white suit guy the only one who has been out here?"

Robie stopped. "Just him." And then jerked his thumb at the pond. "And that feller in there too, I guess."

Bill quickly scanned the area. Who the hell was in the pond? He could see where Price in his covered boots had come up the bank. He saw the thinner, clearer marks and tread of the standard issue patrol boots that Robie wore. Closer to the end of the pond he saw two sets of footprints in the soft sand. He carefully walked over, stopping several feet away. Two sets coming up, one set going back down the slope. One set stopped at the edge of the pond, then two indentations, and a larger one at the very edge of the pond. A couple more, maybe footprints, but dug in and bigger. A shove? A fight? Bill glanced toward the body, his hand up to shade against the glare of the water. It was too far away to I.D., so he carefully retraced his steps and found Robie setting up sawhorses across the path to the pond.

"Who was on last night?"

"Nate had graveyard, but they are just rovers. The run was still on and water was still entering the pond. This was the first check."

Bill snapped his head around like he'd been shot in the neck.

Robie placed the last saw horse. "Nobody from our day shift section, I checked."

Bill lifted his patrol cap and combed through his hair two or three times pressing his palm against his forehead. He squeezed his eyes shut and whispered "shit" under his breath. He stared at Robie for a second before carefully walking around to the end of the pond again, where the body had drifted closer in the current from the unceasing desert wind. He was careful where he placed his steps so as not to disturb any of the earlier prints in the soft sandy soil. As he got closer he slowed and whispered again, "Aw shit, this is bad." Even though face down and still fifty feet away he saw a familiar glint of a silver chain around the neck. The body was of a large husky man, with wavy dark hair, now plastered to his head. It was Nate.

Chapter Three

One call confirmed it. Nate had not checked out after his shift. He had not badged out of the areas. He was not at home, a dumpy little apartment on Jadwin. Bill's second call had been to headquarters to make an official log of the incident and his third call had been to the FBI. He had done all of this from the security office inside the KW building. Robie was back on the gate outside, recording names of anyone who came or went.

He waited and within an hour the FBI in the person of Special Agent Dowd showed up. Agent Dowd had a partner in tow. Through the window he could see them get out of their black government sedan, settle fedoras on their heads and walk towards the door. When they came in they split up, and Dowd came into the little security office.

"So, Rosen, right?" Agent Dowd said when he saw who was sitting behind the desk. "Did you call this in?"

"No. That was Officer Robie Gardener." Bill stopped writing in the security log. "Didn't you get a report from dispatch?"

Dowd looked out the open door of the office, "Yeah, sure. Anyway, we got it from here. Just make sure to keep unauthorized personnel away from the site." Dowd wandered off in search of his partner.

It was 2:00 PM before a flatbed truck with a lead lined box big enough for the body was driven around the pond to where two men in full radiation suits had rowed out in a small boat and brought the body to shore. Bill was standing outside having a smoke when the truck went by heading, he guessed, for town.

Not long after Agent Dowd came walking across the lot towards him. His summer weight suit and hat band were stained with sweat. His shoes were a mess. They always wore shoes, not boots, Bill thought. Right now Dowd looked nervous. He took out a small notebook.

"We got an ID." Dowd said.

"Nate Bourbeau." Bill said.

Dowd looked up. His face was perspiring in the hot afternoon glare. "Why didn't you mention this before?"

"I'm a friend of his and thought I recognized him. Chain around his neck, a St. Christopher medal, right?" Bill looked at the pond where they had fished him out, and across the river to the White Bluffs. "Besides, you didn't really seem interested in my opinion. Plus, I was hoping I was wrong." Bill decided not to mention the calls he had made. He dropped and stubbed out his cigarette. "Where are you taking his body?"

"Sorry Rosen, This is an FBI matter now." Dowd finished writing something in his notebook, flipped it closed, and then adjusted his hat on his head. "No details."

"But what happened? Did he hit his head and fall in?" Bill turned and stared down at Dowd. "The pond is not that deep at the edge." Bill had a couple of inches on Dowd, and looked down at the shorter man.

A faint smile came across Dowd's face, "You a close friend of his?"

"And his Watch Commander when he's not on graveyard." Bill could feel himself heating up.

"I thought you just got that job," Dowd said.

"Officially, but I've been filling in for a couple of months," Bill said.

"But you two were friends, right?" Dowd was in full FBI mode, but it seemed to Bill there was something else going on.

"Yeah, sure. Look I have to get going on the paperwork." Bill turned to leave. "I will get officers to set a perimeter to protect the crime scene."

Dowd stepped in close, grabbed his arm, "We're not saying this is a crime, Rosen and besides what do you know..."

Bill tried to pull away. "Read my file. I was with the Provost's office in Japan. I ran investigations. I got to go."

Dowd did not let go of Bill's arm. "All reports come to our office, Rosen, no duplicates, just originals. Make it simple and leave it to us."

Bill looked down at the hand on his arm, "How's this for simple, get your hand off my arm before I break it."

Dowd stepped back, out of his way, "You're out of this, just remember that."

Bill got in his squad car. Driving off he could see the big truck in the rearview mirror, the gray lead lined box on the back deck. As he passed out the gate, Robie waved him through.

Driving back to headquarters he thought about Nate Bourbeau. Big Nate Bourbeau. They had come on the Hanford Patrol at the same time in '47. Nate was also a vet, had been an MP in the ETO; kept telling Bill about all the money he made on the black market. Money that was always one big score away. Nate did okay on the patrol. It was a lot like MP duty. He was deadly on the gun range, a steady fast shot. He paid enough attention to detail to handle security at any of the sites. He was marked down on his evaluation on deportment, a big deal with the main contractors Dupont and GE who ran Hanford. In other words supervisors and others could tell what he thought of them. There were rumors that he occasionally shook down workers at the site. Sometimes took their contraband booze. Other times he was supposed to have taken money. One thing for certain, Nate did not slip, hit his head, and fall into a cooling pond. Bill frowned, the problem was if people wanted him dead, there were easier ways to do it and hundreds of square miles of empty desert to do it in. He also had a hard time thinking that someone was able to get the drop on Nate.

Chapter Four

Bill spent the rest of the shift with reports. He was careful to place all the reports in a pouch marked FBI. He took his time putting everything together, gathering reports from everyone on the patrol that was even near the B-area that night and the day before.

Officer Frank Richardson came in, walked past his desk and into Bill's office without knocking. Bill didn't look up, tried to keep working and ignored the young officer, hoping he would go away. Bill liked Frank. The young officer was smart, serious about the job and steady as a rock. He was naïve or maybe just green, but he'd get over that.

"Sir, was it Officer Bourbeau?" Bill figured that word would have gotten out fast. Even Frank, who studiously refused to listen to gossip, who would lecture fellow officers on verbal breaches of security could not resist listening to information on the death of a fellow patrolman. Bill still refusing to look at him nodded his head.

"Is it true he was shot?"

Bill jerked up in his chair.

"What? Say that again." Frank took a step back. His face turned pale and then red under his sunburn.

"I realize that this is an improper infraction of procedure." He stammered.

Bill waved his hands dismissively, "Yeah Nate's dead, I was there when they fished him out of the KW pond. What do you mean shot?"

Frank kept moving his patrol hat from one hand to the other. "They brought him to the 300 Area. They had an area in the fabricating labs blocked off. I was detailed to clear the area. There were a lot of people coming and going and I was mostly checking badges. I noticed a couple of docs from the hospital. I was filling out visitor badges even though the Feds wanted to take them right through." Frank looked out the window and waived his hat. "One of them said to the FBI agent, 'GS to the head, are you sure?' The agent looked like he was going to bite his head off but then kind of snatched the badge and shoved the guy down the hall. Is that true Bill? That Nate was shot in the head?" Frank's voice ran down. He looked at Bill like he wanted to say more.

Bill took a sheet of paper and rolled it into the typewriter next to his desk. "Look, thanks for the heads up, but for Christ's sake don't say anything, all right? The Feds are all over my ass on this and they want it to be air-tight. The Feds are good at forensics, all the crime lab stuff, let them handle it."

Frank started to say more. Bill held up a hand, "The Feds will be interviewing everyone and it is going to get tense around here. Just do your job and tell them what you know. Including that you overheard what the doc said."

Bill turned back to the report he was typing. Unlike every other patrolman, Bill could type with both hands and most of his fingers. Frank stood there a moment longer, Bill looked up at him, "Do the job, Frank."

Bill finished at 6:30. He took the pouch with his report and hoped to be able to see Agent Parker when he delivered it to the FBI. Parker was one of the good ones. Not like that useless prick Dowd. Everyone from the day shift was gone. The night Watch Commander was out front in the reception area, going over reports spread out along the long counter. He looked up as Bill passed him on the way out, "Long bad day, Slim."

"Don't need too many of these," Bill said and stepped out into the early summer evening. The sun was still up but long shadows stretched across the gravel lot separating the headquarters from the FBI building. They looked the same, low one story lighter tan, darker tan and made out of wood. Up the three steps and into the building, a young agent sat at the front desk. "I will log in your report, Commander Rosen."

"Is Agent Parker still here?" Bill handed the pouch over to the young agent.

"No sir, he has left for the day." The agent placed the pouch in a drawer that he locked.

Bill got in his truck and headed out. He kept thinking about his next move. He had to see Aggie, let her know what was going on. He figured that the Feds would have told her and probably grilled her on Nate. If the Feds saw this as a murder two things were going to happen: anyone associated with Nate in any way was going to be a suspect and the Feds were going to go into overdrive to keep it quiet.

On the other hand, the FBI didn't like to blow their nose without permission from Washington, so it might be awhile before everything was put off limits. He didn't like it, but the old itch between your shoulders that you could not quite reach, was coming back. He had developed that in Japan, working as a Provost Marshall after the war. Right now he needed to see Nate's apartment.

Bill turned down a side street and headed towards Nate's place. He lived in a crappy little apartment off Jadwin in the north end of town. Originally a men's barracks built for workers during the war, now it was single occupancy apartments. All the apartments were full. Everything was full in this town and people waited on lists for more houses to be built by the government. Bill went through the foyer and down the hall on the first floor to Nate's door. The walls were paper thin, the runner dusty. The place felt close and hot. Bill could hear a man with a smoker's cough in the apartment across from Nate's. Bill tried the door and it was locked. He took the ring of keys from his belt and selected one that looked about the right size. He jiggled it into the lock. The Hanford Patrol and the Village Patrol were given skeleton keys to fit most locks in town and at the project. Bill reflected that it made breaking and entering a much tidier business.

Bill opened the door and found a mess. Nothing unusual, just the usual kind given Nate's personality and gender; he was sloppy, he drank, he smoked, and apparently depended on his sister for the cooking. The small kitchen had dirty dishes in the sink with several pans that looked like they had had casseroles of some kind. The clock above the sink said 7:15. He needed to hurry. There was a coffee pot on the stove; the refrigerator had a bottle of milk, slices of ham, mustard, a couple cans of Hamm's beer and a block of Velveeta. The half counter in the kitchen opened into a small nook off the living room big enough for a small table and two chairs. There was a toaster on it and coffee rings to show where Nate sat. In the living room there was a ratty couch, and a second hand floor model radio. The coffee table contained an overflowing ashtray and a stack of men's magazines. The one on top, *Stag*, showed a scantily dressed blond tied to a stake surrounded by blood dripping head hunters. Off to the side a tousled haired body builder aimed his rifle at the nearest native. "I Saved the Jungle Queen!" Bill shook his head and thought, three years in the jungle and I didn't get to save a single jungle queen. He went into Nate's bedroom, a small hot place with one window, open, the tan drapes moving in the breeze. It was just a single bed, G.I. dresser and a small closet. There was a night stand by the bed, a light with a dusty shade and a drawer. There were a few clothes on the bed, which was made. The closet held a spare Patrol uniform, a suit that looked underused, a couple of shirts and a long overcoat. Not much here, plus I don't know what I am looking for, thought Bill. He opened the drawer of the night stand and saw a small address book. It was mostly empty. Under B were Aggie's address in Richland plus an address in Montana that might have been relatives. Under S there was "Silky" and a number, Springwood 6-1542. Under O there was "Fish" at Whitehall 3-2825. He copied the numbers down in his notebook. He heard someone in the hall outside. Two someones. A murmured conversation and then silence.

Bill put the book back, leaving it for the Feds. He turned and headed for the door. He stopped just inside the bedroom, reached down and eased his pistol out of the holster, holding it slightly behind him. The front door knob turned and started to come open. Bill thumbed back the hammer.

Across the living room the apartment door opened and two men started through, stopped, eyes going wide at Bill, then quickly stepped in and closed the door. They were a real Mutt and Jeff, one beefy, red faced with a nose like a potato, Special Agent Dowd. The other man thin, taller, pencil necked and rattling around inside his double-breasted suit Bill did not know. Dowd reached inside his jacket and pulled out his badge, realizing too late Bill's hand was holding the .45. Pencil Neck just made a small jump as if not trying to be too obvious in stepping behind Dowd.

Bill, always cautious around men with guns and not the sense to use them, slowly holstered his pistol and raised his hands slightly. "Agent Dowd, a pleasure as always."

"I know this joker, name's Rosen." He said to the other agent. "Another one a them Hanford guards."

"Hanford Patrol." Bill said.

"Well Mister Patrol, what are you doing here?" Dowd nodded to his partner as if to say "Gotcha."

His partner smiled slightly as he leaned against the couch, took off his hat and dropped it on a cushion. "This apartment is off limits and related to an accident at the Hanford Site."

This guy had to be new in town. Nobody called it the Hanford Site. Just Hanford, or more likely, The Plant. FBI agents rotated in and out of Richland. There were as many as 20 to 25 in town at any one time, but just a few, like Agent Parker, and useless dumb asses, like Dowd, were permanent. Pencil Neck would probably go on to other posts, he was sharp.

Bill folded his arms, "You mean the accident where Nate Bourbeau shot himself in the back of the head?" Dowd and Pencil Neck went still and quiet. It was interesting to see the contrast between the two men. Pencil Neck cocked his head and shifted back on his heels. Dowd's face changed to the color of his hair, red brown and blotchy.

"Sit down asshole." Dowd took a step forward. "We got a few questions, the first being how do you know so much?"

Bill looked at Pencil Neck but said to Dowd, "You gotta read your reports, Dowd. I got called in, I was the first supervisor on the scene."

"Yeah I remember our little conversation but they didn't fish him out till after you left. And there was nothing in the report about foul play."

"Foul play, crimony, Dowd, you sound like the Shadow." Bill turned one of the kitchen chairs around and straddled it, resting his elbows on the back.

Pencil Neck had leaned back against the sofa, "Regardless of the nature of this incident, the FBI is very concerned about security, making sure that rumors or even facts of this case are not released."

"Pardon me, where are my manners, I'm Bill Rosen, day shift Watch Commander of the Hanford Patrol. Now, excuse me, but in the name of security, who are you?" Bill stuck out his hand and put on his best winning smile. Dowd's face got three shades darker but Pencil Neck smiled and stuck out his hand.

"Special Agent Jennings. Glad to meet you Commander Rosen. Would you mind telling us what you saw today? I know it is all in the report you will be sending us, but telling it again fresh?" He smiled back, straight white teeth, light hair neatly cut and parted perfectly on the side. Steel rimmed glasses gave him a serious look.

Bill smiled and thought this was one cool customer. "Sure, although there is not much to say. I came on shift just an hour before. I was on my way to the 200 Area for a shift check, when I was radioed and sent to 100 F."

"Were you at the 200 Area?" Jennings had pulled out a notebook and was consulting it.

"No, north of the 300 area, by the old high school."

"High school?"

"Brick shell by the river, mile or so north of the 300 Area. Anyway, a floater had been spotted by the radiation monitor who contacted the building site security officer. When the officer, that was Officer Robie Gardener, got to the scene he first thought it might have been a deer, but when he climbed the berm he saw that it was a body."

"Did he try to retrieve the body?" Jennings tapped a pen against his notepad.

"No, the monitor told him a hot flush had been made in the last eight hours. It was way too hot, plus face down and no movement." Bill said.

"Still, shouldn't he have tried to get him, just to be sure?" Jennings at this point had completely excluded Dowd.

Bill rubbed his eyes, thought about reaching for a cigarette. "How long you been here?"

"What do you mean?" Jennings stopped tapping his pen.

"I mean Richland, Hanford. How long you been here?" Bill said.

Jennings shook his head, his smile gone. "That's Bureau business."

"Okay, maybe not long. Look Jennings, that's not a fishing pond. These are single pass plutonium production reactors. The water comes into the core and keeps the whole thing from melting and then out to the ponds. It cools and settles and then back to the river. Every now and then they add a caustic compound and flush the whole reactor while it's operating to clean it out; it's called a hot flush. When it comes out it is very radioactive, full of lots of nasty stuff. Anybody face down in the retention ponds is dead. Period." Bill reached for a cigarette lighting one off his Zippo.

Dowd started to say something but Jennings cut him off. "How'd you know about the gunshot wound? I don't even think the autopsy is finished."

Bill took a drag off his cigarette, slowly stood, flexing his bum knee, "Doc Stillman is the medical examiner doing the autopsy, right? Big guy, loud voice, likes to hear himself talk? He was talking to one of your guys while we were getting him a badge. I got some smart boys."

Dowd broke in, "I want the names of those officers now. I want them suspended and isolated."

Bill tapped his cigarette in Nate's full ashtray, "I don't remember their names. It's what I know. What I told you. That's as far as it goes. We are just sitting around a dead guy's apartment chatting. I'm leveling with you, but if you get pissy, I'll shut up."

"I'll tell you when to shut up. We have jurisdiction here. We investigate murders here. You don't investigate shit."

Jennings, ignoring Dowd, "You and Nate close friends?"

"Not really. We came on at the same time, trained together and were on the same shifts for a few years. We'd have a few beers after work sometimes." Bill said

"You talk politics?" Jennings said.

"You mean Ike vs. Stevenson?"

"You know what I mean." Jennings was back tapping his pen.

Bill walked to the window, moved the curtain, looked out at the fading light, turned, "You mean was he pink? Christ no. Nate was brown. Full of bullshit."

"You know he has a sister?" Jennings said.

"Let me think, maybe." Bill let the curtain drop turned and faced them.

"You know her. What do you think of her?" Jennings.

Bill shook his head. He was trying to be careful. "Think of her? Maybe Nate said she worked here. Real smart."

"You two date?" Jennings, still with his level voice.

"I don't think I'd be her type. I'm not a college boy like you Jennings. Maybe you should look her up."

Jennings gave it a short laugh, holding up his hands, taking it as a joke. "Okay, okay. Just trying to get a picture here."

"Picture this. Nate's dead with a bullet in his skull." Bill looked at his watch. "You know and I know he has a sister; who's probably tore up right now."

Dowd had his own notebook out now, "What kind of gun do you carry, Rosen?

Bill reached to his holster and drew his pistol in one fluid motion. Dowd and Jennings flinched, but Bill slid the magazine out and jacked back the slide, popping out the round in the chamber. Ignoring Dowd, he handed it butt first to Jennings. "Government Issue Model 1911A Browning .45 auto."

Jennings took the clean and smoothly oiled pistol. "This isn't standard for the Patrol, is it?"

"No," Bill said, "But I have permission to carry it."

"What is the regulation firearm for the Hanford Patrol?" Jennings asked.

"Sidearm is a .38 Special. We also have Tommy guns and riot guns, BARs and some 30 oughts with scopes. But you know all that." Bill had enough of these two. They were just backfilling information but Bill wanted out. He looked at his watch again, 7:35.

"Do you have a .38 special issued to you by the patrol?" Jennings said.

"No. I had one but they let me turn it back in last year." Bill began to think they might know something after all. What do they like about a .38?

"Do you own any other guns?" Jennings said.

"Sure, a 30-30 and a 16 gauge pump, a couple of bazooka's and an ack-ack gun on the roof of my house." Bill picked up his hat and headed toward the door. He stopped at the threshold and turned, "And no I didn't shoot Nate with any of them. He was a friend, a pain in the ass sometimes, but not so much to shoot him and dump him in a cooling pond." He held out his hand for his sidearm. Jennings returned it.

Dowd, consulting his notebook, "Tomorrow come down and check with us at 10:00 sharp. We will take a more formal statement then."

Jennings had unbuttoned his jacket, a cool summer weight gray flannel. He flapped it saying, "Sure stays hot here."

Bill ignored the atmospheric comment. "You've got a problem." He pocketed the loose round and slipped the magazine back into the pistol with a snap. "Keeping a lid on this."

"So what's your point?" Jennings had dropped all pretense of involving Dowd.

Bill waived at the clock on the wall, "Not a lot of time."

"Right, Officer Rosen. See you tomorrow, ten." Jennings said

Bill pulled open the door, "So aren't you going to ask me the question?"

Jennings had buttoned his jacket, "OK, I'll bite. Officer Rosen, do you know who shot Officer Bourbeau?"

"No, and I don't have the slightest idea."

Chapter Five

By 8:45 Bill was back in the truck and heading out. Bill knew about twenty guys that would be glad Nate was dead. Nate was more than a pain in the ass, he was a trouble maker. He would go out of his way to needle someone. He was intensely competitive, loud, a show off, would bet on anything and had no trouble cheating. He loved to play poker, craps, and ponies, often took his two weeks' vacation and went to Reno or Santa Anita. He would disappear for long weekends to Portland, gambling and whoring. Bill would see him when he returned, nursing a massive hangover, glaring evilly at anyone who dared talk to him. He could never quit while he was ahead. For Nate it was always about winning the next hand, never being satisfied that he had enough. So sure, Bill knew lots of people who wouldn't mind seeing him dead. He just didn't know anyone who would blow his brain's out and dump him in a reactor pond.

He got behind one of the gray and tan buses heading for the north barricade. Full of workers it wallowed along, black diesel smoke coming out of the upright exhaust. He had to slow down. He wanted to go home. It had been a long weird day, and tomorrow would be longer. Still, he had to see the one person who truly loved Nate, his big sister, Aggie.

Bill turned east on Van Geisen and crossed George Washington Way. Aggie lived on Newcomer, just a block from the river in a Q house. Unlike most of Richland, it was a quiet, shady area, with cool breezes coming off the river. Her house was government built and about the same size as everyone else's, but these homes were better sited, had better construction and were unofficially reserved for the top administrators and scientists.

Bill pulled to the curb in front of her place behind a black 1950 Ford sedan. He got out and walked up the steps. At that moment the door opened and Agent Parker, hat in hand came out, followed by Aggie, head down, hands together, nodding. Thank god it was Parker, Bill thought. The FBI agent glanced at Bill, turned back to Aggie.

As Bill came up the steps he heard Agent Parker, "Again, I am sorry for your loss, you have my number and if there is anything you think might help us out give me a call." He put his hat on and walked down the steps past to Bill. Parker, neat in a dark suit that looked sharp even in the heat, stopped, shook his hand and said, "Call me tonight. Important."

Aggie was standing on the small landing twisting a handkerchief. She was wearing a short-sleeved white cotton blouse and blue slacks. Her dark hair was pulled back; a few strands fell loose over her face. Her eyes were red. She saw Bill and her face twisted and her voice clutched, "Oh, Bill, they said Nate was killed and you were there." She went into his arms, her head against his shoulder, crying. She gripped him and sobbed. He held her and felt her shaking, felt her grief. In the quiet neighborhood a passing car slowed, a young couple staring at the Hanford patrolman holding a woman whose cries could be heard in the street.

After a while she pulled back, took her handkerchief and blew her nose long and loud. Without saying anything she took Bill by the hand and guided him inside. She sat on the overstuffed sofa in the living room and pulled her feet up. She cried softly. He sat in an old wingback chair across from her. He started to say something, stopped. Her sobs slowly subsided into hiccups. Bill could see her body relax, sat back, blew her nose again and wiped her eyes.

"I guess I need to make arrangements. Oh god, he's dead, how could this happen? Call Einan's and see about the, the body, oh god he's really dead. The church. Why Bill? Why? Father Ryan called already." Her words trailed off and she slumped across the couch.

Bill sat forward, reached across and held her hand. Squeezed it and let go. He sat back. She had the twisted handkerchief up to her mouth. "I don't..., stay, please?"

"Sure kid." The dark outside was complete. The front door was open. The windows in the tiny living room let in the evening breeze. He heard a dog bark and a car door slam. One light was on in the hallway, the rest of the house dark. She faded into the shadows. Bill sat. His watch glowed, 10:25. He could hear soft breathing.

He sat. Finally he got up and moved to her side, draping the afghan over her that had been on the back of the couch. He thought about getting a pillow. Let it go, he thought, this is enough. He sat. She had said her folks were gone. Now her brother. He thought of his own mother, who died when he was 15. He remembered his father and brother, and the hole it had left in their lives.

Midnight. He must have dozed. The glowing hands on his watch stood straight. Aggie slept on the couch, still on her side, her hands folded under her cheek. The curtains were billowing in front of the open windows. He stood, a spike of pain in his knee, something else creaked and popped. He thought about getting her a pillow, but didn't want to go into her bedroom to get it. Closing the front door gently behind him, he walked out into the warm evening, the wind picking up, blowing from the west.

It was just a few blocks to uptown. On the corner was a low brown brick building with the letters VFW on the outside. He parked close and walked inside. Along one side was a long bar with two groups of two men. They had drinks, maybe had come off swing shift and stopped in for a bump. He waived at the bartender who nodded. He went to the back to the pay phone, dropped in a nickel and called Agent Parker.

"Agent Parker," he said with only a trace of sleep in his voice.

"Look, sorry, but you said to call." Bill said

"Not a problem." Parker hesitated, "There's something you need to know. The Bureau is seeking information on you."

"You mean I'm a suspect?" Bill looked out at the mostly empty bar. Two of the men were laughing.

"Not really. A couple of things have turned up. The main one is that Nate may have been selling secrets to the Reds. And if that's the case this thing just became a whole lot bigger, and anyone with any knowledge of that is culpable." Parker said all of this in a neutral tone.

"Holy Christ. They can't have any evidence." Bill said. "Nate's a screw-up, but not treason, I just can't see it."

"They can. They have part of something. It has to do with money. You wouldn't know anything about that would you?" Parker said.

Bill thought of the Ford, the men and Nate being flush, "Sounds like you're fishing."

Parker went on, "If it's there we'll find it. You know the boys from D.C. are going to crawl all over this and they'll pin it on someone. But here is the other thing, and I'm going way out on a limb here. Do you know about the gray list workers?"

Bill thought for a second, "You mean like Von Braun and the other Nazis brought over after the war?"

Parker hesitated, "We've got them here too."

Bill, juggling the phone against his shoulder got his cigarettes out and lit one. Sitting in the little wooden half booth was making his back ache. "No kidding. Look, just for the record, I don't know what Nate was up to but I intend to find out."

"No." Parker's voice was calm but final.

"I'm not asking permission." Bill said.

"Bill, you're making it tough on me. It's a Bureau matter. Really, stay away. Your little stunt this afternoon has already rung bells in our office, probably all the way back to D.C. Everybody is keeping a close eye on this." Parker said. "If you go too far out on a limb, there will nothing I can do. Are we clear on that?"

Bill sat for a moment, stretched his knee, trying to decide what he wanted to say to Parker, Finally he said, "Yeah, sure. There's two ways this goes, either the mug who got Nate is still here, or it was a pro job. If he's a pro he's gone and maybe your boys can get him, maybe. But I'm not going to stop on this end. Present company excepted, the crew downtown couldn't find their own asses with both hands and a flashlight."

There was a long moment on the phone, and then Parker said, "Okay Rosen, it's your funeral."

Chapter Six

Bill had the gritty jazzed up high of too many cigarettes, too much coffee and not enough sleep when he reported for his shift the next morning. Everybody there was walking on eggshells. Everyone had a black armband and Howard, a normally loud and easy going Georgian, was cutting pieces of black electricians tape to put on badges. Howard looked more serious doing that than at any time Bill had known him. He looked up as Bill headed for his office. "A word boss?"

Bill motioned him back to his office. Selma had placed a neat stack of messages on his desk, most from the FBI. Bill placed his hat on the rack and sat down. "Okay, shoot."

"Well, first I want you to know that I am real sorry about what happened. Nate and I didn't see eye to eye all the time, but he was one of us, and it makes me so damn mad to think of him shot and dumped in that pond. When we catch that son of a bitch."

"Whoa, slow down Howard." He motioned him to sit. "You know we gotta be real calm about all this."

Howard sat; all big legs, big frame, big arms. "Yeah well anyway, I got something I want to tell you. I hear the FBI will be talking to everyone and all, and I have something you need to hear, maybe before they do. You know that juke joint on 14th in east Pasco, the Diamond Club?"

Bill started to shift through the messages, "Sure, best ribs in the Tri-Cities. Good place for jazz and the occasional knife fight. Honestly, Howard, aren't you a deacon in the Baptist church?"

"Well, you know a man has to have ribs every now and then."

Bill put down the messages, "Howard, are you sure it's the ribs and not the chocolate?"

"Look boss, I'm a family man." Howard sat back, looking genuinely offended, "Do you want to know what I got or not?"

Bill said, "I do, and I don't want to know what you are doing when you tell Betty you are working a double shift."

Howard was starting to get red. He cleared his throat and continued, "I was there a couple of weeks ago, Saturday late, and I saw Nate. I didn't think much of it cuz I've seen him at the Diamond Club before. One of the girls that works at the place was with him and there was this other guy. He really stuck out, looked uncomfortable. They all seemed to be getting along. But then Nate saw me and just shook his head like I wasn't supposed to know him."

Howard stopped for a minute, "That was the odd part. Nate was always so full of himself that if he saw you he would always come over and get you to buy him a drink. But not this time."

"Who was the other guy?"

"Not sure." Howard scrubbed the top of his head. "Bet he works at the plant though. Maybe late thirties, stocky, brush cut."

Before lunch Bill went to Kadlec Hospital. He needed to find Doc Stillman. He found him coming out of the maternity ward in his wrinkled white coat, tie and black pants, stethoscope around his neck, carrying a metal clipboard.

He squinted at Bill's uniform, eyes red rimmed. "Uh, officer, what can I do for you?"

"Hey Doc, Bill Rosen" He stuck out a hand.

"Oh right. Patella, shattered if I remember right. You got that in the Pacific, right. Did the exercises help?" He was walking and making notes on his clipboard. More to himself he said, "I should have paid more attention as an intern to OB. Sorry, what can I do for you?"

"You did the autopsy on Nate Bourbeau?"

The doctor stopped, shook his head, "Wouldn't know, FBI matter." He tapped the metal chart he was holding.

Bill had taken off his hat, twirled it once or twice, "Okay, I'm just asking, you know, for the family. About the disposition of the body."

Doc Stillman kept tapping the metal chart. "It's an FBI matter. I don't believe the body will be released.

Doc Stillman looked around. "You should look at the records we have on that knee of yours. We keep complete records."

"Look Doc, the knee's fine." They were standing in front of a large office with the sign 'records' over the door. Inside, Bill could see a woman at a desk in front of a bank of file cabinets. A nurse was filing charts in the back.

"I've got to get back to rounds. Look up what we have on that knee of yours." Doc Stillman walked off shaking his head.

Bill ducked into the office. He flashed a smile and then pointed to his badge, "How're you this morning? Doc Stillman said I should read my file on my bum knee." He pointed to his leg and made a face, clowning, "Guess he's busy."

The trim young woman at the desk in front of him looked at his badge, his leg, smiled, "Looks pretty good to me."

"Looks ain't everything. Plus I'm old."

"Doc Stillman is too busy for his own good." She made a frown, "What's the name?"

"Rosen, Bill. It was last May when I saw him." She had already gotten up, giving it a little extra as she moved along the bank of files.

She pulled the file and returned it to him. "You can't take this out of here. The files need to stay."

"Yeah, sure." He pulled up a chair, made a show of getting out his notebook. The clock hit 12:00. The receptionist and the other woman grabbed purses and headed for the door. The receptionist stopped, turned, "You can come back later if you want."

"There's just a little more I need. Tell you what, I'll leave it on your desk when I go, pull the door shut. How's that?"

"I don't know." She looked out the hall. The other woman started to walk away.

"Go to lunch. Anybody says anything, I'll arrest them."

"Promise?" she laughed, white teeth against red lips.

He moved down the row of cabinets after she left. He could look out into the hall to see if anyone was there. He hauled open several file drawers until he found Nate's folder.

It didn't look like much. The first few pages were history. Notations from several years back including a shot for penicillin, with the notation VD. Then there were the last pages. One page showed the outline of a man. Several handwritten notes included GSW to the head and arrows to denote where the bullet entered and exited. Chemical burns on 70% of the body. Blistering and rupturing of the skin. There were three large black and white pictures. In one Nate is on his back, on a table or slab, his face bubbled and cracked, dark, burnt. His chest exposed most of the front of the shirt dissolved and in tatters. The second showed Nate on his side, two men in full radiation gear propping him up. The shot is from overhead. His front showed the effects of being in the toxic pond, the back relatively normal, except the messy back of his head where the bullet emerged, taking part of his skull with it. A flap of scalp hung down exposing white bone and bloody gray matter. The last photo was a close-up of his head, from the front. The neat round hole in his forehead above the ruined face, the muscles in the jaw had slackened, the burned and scarred mouth open, almost a leer, a laugh. Nate.

Later that day after work Bill drove south out of town towards Kennewick along the marshes, past the point where the muddy brown Yakima joined the blue Columbia. He turned onto the bridge and into Pasco. A rail and market center before the war, the town was a transportation hub in the eastern part of the state. Served by major highways and passenger rail, it was often the first look people got coming to work at Hanford. Pasco and Kennewick, along with Richland, had become the Tri-Cities. All three supported the Hanford Project to some degree. Pasco had a reputation as a tough little town, made even more so by recent events. During the war African Americans were recruited to work on the Hanford project. They worked many jobs including skilled trades, construction and other jobs building the reactors, processing labs and other infrastructure. These were good paying jobs with good wages paid at roughly the same scale as their white co-workers. The government didn't like non-whites living in the government housing in Richland.

Anytime a black worker would put his name on the housing board, it would not come up. They gravitated to east Pasco where rents and the social climate was more amenable. Soon there was a thriving African American community in Pasco.

After the war, however, they were the first to be laid off as production slowed. With men returning from the war, a veteran's preference rule was enforced, putting ex-service men at the head of the line. As a consequence, as Bill knew, many of the people in East Pasco were poor and stuck.

Bill drove east and turned north on the highway leading to Ritzville and Spokane. Just past the city limits he came to a long low white clapboarded building surrounded by a large gravel parking lot. A sign on a pole in the parking lot announced, "Diamond's Ribs, music, dancing." Bill parked among the few cars in the lot. These would be families, here for take-out, not wanting to heat up their houses on a warm evening. Later, the music would tune up, the talk would get louder and the drinks would get stronger. The place would be packed.

He walked inside and sat at a table. The restaurant in the front held tables and wood paneling in a cowboy theme. Through swinging doors he could just see into the dark bar in the back. Through the serving window wafted the smell of hickory smoked ribs, brisket and chicken. Through the window Bill heard the deep rumble of Tiny 'Diamond' Tule's voice.

"Captain Slim. Good to see you." He emerged out of the kitchen, dressed in chef's whites, splattered here and there with rib sauce. He sat at Bill's table, the chair straining under his weight. Six four or five and a good three hundred, Tiny wiped his hand and shook Bill's.

"Kind of early for you Captain?"

"Actually, I'm on business." Bill frowned, considering how much he wanted to tell Tiny. "You know Nate Bourbeau?"

"Yeah, you and him and that sweet sister of his come in here, what, once or twice?" He leaned back, his hand over his mouth. "She liked the food; don't know if she liked the atmosphere. Nate comes in too much, drinks too much, gambles in the back too much. Bothers the girls too much."

"Well, he's dead. Out at the project so I'm part of the investigation, sort of."

"Uh-huh. So do I know anything? Well the FBI did come by about an hour ago and asked about him in a roundabout way. They didn't tell me he was dead. I already knew that. Word travels fast."

"Who came by?"

"You know they always come in pairs. Skinny sharp dude and a dumpy one in a bad suit. You know 'em?"

"That would be Jennings and Dowd." Bill nodded. "FBI with their usual style."

"Whatever. They asked a lot of questions about Nate, how many times did he come in here, did he see anyone, that sort of thing. I told them I knew him as a customer."

"Right. Did you tell them you held his markers for cards?"

"Hell no. They asked about Silky. Told them the girls who worked here sometimes used fake names to keep customers from getting too fresh."

"Did they buy it?"

"No. They had her number from somewhere. They had checked her house and found out she worked here."

"So where is Connie?"

"She heard about what happened and got scared and was staying with her aunt. She's coming by in a little while to collect her pay on her way out of town."

"Why's she skipping town?

"Not sure. See, she heard that Nate was shot. Right then she decided to leave. Guess she didn't need the trouble."

"Why didn't you tell this to the FBI?"

"Those two? Look, I don't need that kind of trouble. I don't want no part of anything that's going on out there. Nate was okay for a white boy but lots of people could see something like this happening." Tiny said.

"What do you mean?" Bill again had that feeling that there were more threads to what had happened.

"Me? I don't know nothing. All I see is more people comin' in, more work, more secrets. More money. Too much of that and boys like Nate start to think they can get a piece of it. Like I said, I don't know nothin', and Nate, for all his talk, kept his business close."

"When is Connie due in?" Bill said sitting back.

"She said she'd be by, soon I expect. Get yourself a plate of brisket, Captain, you look like you could use it." Tiny heaved himself up, disappeared back behind the counter and into the kitchen.

Bill had finished his supper and was on his second cigarette when she came in. Connie, "Silky" Wallace, turned heads wherever she went. Tall, slim, in her late twenties, elegant features and coffee colored skin. She saw Bill and smiled and then hesitated and went into the kitchen to find Tiny. A little later she came out. She had on a tan checked traveling suit.

She stopped by his booth, sat. "Bill, I guess you know I heard about Nate."

"So Connie, are you going to be alright?" Bill said in a soft voice.

"No, not really. I liked Nate. He was always sweet to me." This she said in a small voice. Her eyes started to water. "How's his sister, Aggie?"

"She's in a pretty bad way." Maybe Nate and Connie were closer than he knew.

Nate had mentioned her. She was a cocktail waitress but also served as a dealer in the card room in the back.

"Look, I gotta go. The train leaves in an hour." she said.

"Before you go, can you tell me anything? What was Nate up to?

She smiled, sad, "You know how he was, full of plans. He was worried though. About a month ago he said he had a big score coming, but then he just got quiet. Told me anything happened to him to leave, pronto. I owe him that much, to take his advice." She gathered up her purse

Bill got to his feet, walked with her towards the door, "Anything else?"

"I think he was in over his head, whatever it was. He didn't deserve that. Not Nate." She put her head down, "I gotta go," she pushed out into the early evening. A cab was waiting for her.

Chapter Seven

Josef Ososkie woke to the sound of banging and children screaming next door. The shades were drawn and the windows closed in his small duplex. It was 3:30 in the afternoon, scorching in the August afternoon sun and heat. Kids ran through the neighborhood, playing cowboys and Indians, cops and robbers or army and aliens. Swarming through the houses, ignoring the 'Day Sleeper' sign he had put prominently in the front window. For the hundredth time he said that as soon as possible he needed to find somewhere else to live.

His little place worked for him, even with the Manolo's next door. They were a large Italian family that was adding new members every year. Buddy Manolo was from Lowell, Massachusetts where he had worked for Remington Arms. He had taken a job with Du Pont and moved to Hanford in '43. During the war he worked as a machinist, mostly cutting graphite to very fine tolerances for the reactor piles. Now he supervised the milling of plutonium into the exotic shapes necessary for the latest weapons. At heart, Buddy was a family man. After the war Buddy took his savings and went to Verona Italy. He returned with a wife, ten years younger than him, 19 years old. That was in 1948.

Josef could now hear Maria's (Misses Manolo's) voice as she yelled at the children, "Outside with all of you, and quit making so much noise, let the poor man next door get some sleep!" The noise abated for a moment and then the doors banged as the children ran out the back. Maria was solicitous of Josef. She was a dark eyed beauty who felt isolated in this desert town, surrounded by strangers. She was a member of the alter committee at Christ the King Church, but did not get along with the other ladies on the committee. She confided to Josef that she did not really care for Father Ryan. He was, well, Irish. All of this had been related to Josef while he relit the oil furnace in her basement. She was then, as now, pregnant, and could not bend down to hit the reset switch. She had found out he was Polish and Catholic, and treated him like a long lost relative. She would say to him, "You know how it is, these people" and then roll her eyes and take a drag on her cigarette. She loved Buddy, in her way, but was continually pestering him to bring over more of her family. Buddy, devoted to his wife, tried to accommodate her.

Meanwhile, Josef was just trying to get some sleep. He worked graveyard as a chemist in the Purex Building. He supervised operators in the separation facility, using remote equipment to take slugs of enriched uranium and dissolve them to recover the tiny amounts of plutonium. This was a middle step in the process of turning uranium into weapons grade material. He liked his job, plus, it did not take much effort on his part. The work at this point was mostly routine. Many of the operators had been with the project since the forties. Even with the new projects and increased production, more safeguards were in place. The new projects meant more plutonium.

The future looked bright for Josef. He was a polish refugee who had been plucked from a labor camp and transported to Peenemunde on the Pomeranian coast during the war. He had worked for the Nazi's making V2 rockets. After the war he had made his way west, determined to avoid falling into the hands of the Red Army. He had been picked up by the U.S. Army and turned over to agents from the American OSS, who were scouring the newly liberated Germany for just such men. After giving them his papers and undergoing debriefing for weeks, he had been moved to a series of camps; ultimately being transported to the United States. Unfortunately his knowledge of rockets was minimal and he was not able to work with Von Braun in California. He was offered and accepted a job at Hanford, where his knowledge of chemical and industrial organization was put to use. Under a special program, he was given an accelerated date for his citizenship.

He didn't mind working the graveyard shift, 11:00 pm to 7:00 AM. In the summer the nights were cooler than the scorching days. The heat of the day would slowly subside, giving way to silky warm desert nights, cool by 2:00 in the morning when he would take his lunch box and sit outside. Moonlight would turn the desert silvery gray; Rattlesnake Mountain resting in the near distance. The long canyon of the Purex Building, like some gray concrete ship marooned in the sand and sagebrush would stretch out before him five stories high and longer than three football fields. Some workers had hammered together a picnic table out of scrap lumber. Overhead large power lines, big enough to light up a small city, snaked into the building.

So different from where he was born, a little apartment above a shop in Cracow, where mother, father and sister lived and where father everyday would go downstairs to the haberdashery shop that he owned. His life had been very ordered then, school and home, summers to see relatives in the countryside, the green rolling hills and winding rivers heading east into dark forests. Later he was in University, where he found that his sense of order suited the field of Chemistry. He had gotten along with his professors and had even begun work on an article when the war came, the Germans smashing through the Polish cities in the first wave of the Blitzkrieg. Within a year Josef was in a labor camp, his father dead, shot outside his shop. His mother and sister both disappeared into the Nazi work camps. He had first just been a common laborer, but when they found out he had university training as a chemist he was shipped north, ending up at Peenemunde on the coast of the North Sea, assembling the V2 rockets that would soon be launched against the British. He was always amused at the American view that Germans worked with unerring efficiency. His own firsthand experience was that working in one of the advanced German laboratories was more of a slapdash operation than anything the Americans would tolerate. Here in this great desert of the American West no expense was being spared to put together and safely protect workers engaged in the astounding process of creating fundamentally new elements. He thanked god that Hitler never had access to such material.

But now he was troubled. He had heard about the Hanford patrol officer that some said was killed. He remembered what happened last week. It was here, outside the Purex building having his lunch that he heard angry voices, first in English, then in German, then in badly spoken German and finally in English again. He could not make out the words, but into the light at the front of the building from the parking lot he could see two men walking, both angry, one stopping to push the other by the shoulder. One of them was a Hanford patrol officer, and the other was Miller. They saw him, one pointed and they both came toward him.

The Hanford patrol officer, a large man with dark hair and his cap pulled low over his eyes, shined a large flashlight in his direction. Josef had started to put his lunch remains back in his bucket when the officer said, "Hold up there a second, bud. You're Ososkie, right?"

The two men came and stood next to the table. Ososkie looked from one to the other. "Yes, Officer, is there a problem?"

The tall officer sat down. The other man remained standing. He was dressed like Josef, work pants and short sleeved shirt. A badge clipped to his shirt pocket indicated he worked in the 200 West Area. The officer took off his hat, dropped it on the table. Ignoring Josef's question he said, "I just love these nights, cools off, let's you get a break from the heat. You like working graveyard?"

Ososkie did not know what to say, "Excuse me?"

The officer leaned forward, spoke slowly, "Do you like working graveyard?"

Ososkie had no idea what was going on. "Sure, like you said, it's better than days out here."

The officer looked at the other man, "Did I say it was better than days?" He shook his head, "I don't believe I said anything about days or swing shift for that matter. I just asked a simple question, making conversation. Here's another simple question, you like your job?"

Ososkie was getting angry, "What do you mean?"

The officer looked at the other man again, "You see, you see what we have to work with? Ask a couple of real simple questions and nothing but static."

The other man sat down next to Ososkie, the makeshift table creaking with his weight. He turned and faced Ososkie and said in faintly accented English, "What's the matter Josef, can't you be polite?"

The officer broke in, "Forget it Hank. He doesn't look like the type who wants to play ball. Guess we'll have to let the FBI know he is uncooperative." He started to get up.

Ososkie looked between the two men, "Uncooperative, FBI, wait a minute, I'm not uncooperative! You haven't asked anything."

The other man, Hank, motioned to the officer, "Give us a minute, okay?"

Hank put his elbows on the table and watched the patrol man walk off, towards the entrance of the long building. He was solidly built, his shoulders pressed tight against the shirt he was wearing. Josef could see the line of an old scar that disappeared into his neatly trimmed hair. He turned to Josef and spoke to him in German, "This is some kind of world, eh? You and me sitting out here in the night in the Wild West. We even have a cowboy looking after us."

Josef did not know what to say. He had seen this man around town and knew he worked in the area. He had thought he might be one of the German scientists brought over after the war. His appearance and his accent seemed to betray that. "I only speak English now." Josef said.

Hank switched to English, "Whatever. I'm going to tell you straight. You have two days to get us information on who you are working with that is giving information to the Russians. We know you know someone who works here who is passing information to the Reds. How's my English?"

Startled, Josef began to rise. Hank placed a strong hand on his forearm and sat him back down. "You're not going anywhere." He kept his hand on Josef's forearm, squeezing slightly.

Josef said to the man holding on to him, "What are you talking about. I don't know anything. I work in processing, that's it."

"Come on, a sneaky little Pole like you, sure you know someone who talks, writes home. Think hard. We'll be in touch." With that, the man got up, patted

Josef on the shoulder, and said, "You don't want to disappoint the FBI, do you?"

The Hanford patrolman had come back, and the two men nodded at each other. The officer pointed his finger at Josef, pistol style, "Thanks for your cooperation on this important matter." They turned and went back to the front parking lot, got in the patrolman's car and drove off. After a minute the warm night quieted Josef's racing thoughts.

And now it was a week later. He hadn't heard from the men, and he had not done anything. He had decided not to go to the authorities for fear of losing his job. He had decided to just deny them anything and take the consequences. This was America, you could do that and things would be fine.

Chapter Eight

Bill had slept hard. The events of the last two days had caught up with him. He had awoken at 6:00 showered and was making coffee, putting together a couple of spam sandwiches and a banana for lunch. This afternoon there would be a memorial service for Nate, held at Christ the King. The body would not be there and there had been no word of a grave site service. A good portion of the off duty and on duty Patrol would be in attendance. The Tri-City Herald had put in a small notice of the memorial. There was a page six notice that an officer had died on the Hanford reservation. No mention of an ongoing investigation or suspicions of murder. Anything that happened at Hanford was government business, and government business was off limits.

Bill had poured the last of his coffee into his thermos. His phone rang, Special

Agent Parker, "Come to my office on your way in. You've got another one."

Agent Parker was standing outside the FBI office when Bill pulled into the lot. Parker got into the cab of the truck and said, "Go down to the park, I've something I want you to see."

They pulled into the small lot at the end of Lee Blvd., and walked along the fence by the river. The Columbia River flowed smooth and serene in the warm morning. The trees overhead formed a canopy, providing cool shade. The trees here were at least 30 years old, tall locusts and cottonwoods, forming a cool space, dappled with morning light. The Riverside Park was part of the original town of Richland, a small farm community that was scraped off to make way for the new government town planted on top of it. They stopped at a bench and Parker handed Bill a folder. Inside were four large glossy photos, showing a man sprawled on the ground, face down, blood pooling underneath his head. The first photo was a close-up, the others showed orientation. Bill recognized the Russian olive trees of the shelter-belt on the west side of town.

"So who was he?" Bill said, squinting at the photos, trying to recognized him.

"Chemist named Ososkie. Polish ref that worked in 221-T. Supervising operators. Real quiet life apparently, good neighbor, Catholic, single, background clean as a whistle. Worked graveyard, got off work last night, passed out of the area but never made it home. Couple of kids came out there to play found him. The Richland Village Police showed up and called us. You know him?"

"No, I might have seen him if he was in the 300 Area but I don't recognize him." Bill looked through the file and saw a copy of Ososkie's badge photo. He nodded his head. "Wait, yeah, he's been here awhile, I used to see him outside at night with his lunch. He kidded me about being a real cowboy. Nice guy." People came to Hanford from all over the country and the really smart ones from all over the world. He looked at the authorization on the badge sheet. "He was in the same area as Nate."

"I noticed that also. Did Nate know him or ever mention him?" Parker said.

"He never said anything to me. Besides he looks like a real straight arrow, not one of Nate's usual friends. Looks like the only thing they had in common was the killer." Bill looked at Parker for confirmation.

"Maybe, maybe not. Gunshot wound to the head. Could have been suicide." Parker said.

"I don't see a weapon." Bill said, holding one photo up close, looking at the area around the man.

"There wasn't one when the Patrol showed up. Look closer, look at his phone number. It's the same as the one written down in the address book Nate kept by his bed. I know you saw it if you were in Nate's apartment, which you were, because agents Dowd and Jennings saw you there. So let me ask you again, did Nate ever mention him?" Agent Parker looked at Bill as if weighing whether to believe his answer.

Bill shook his head, "This is all news to me."

Agent Parker took back the file from Bill and tapped it on his leg. "That's what I figured. Anyway, this thing just took a bad turn. Dowd is about to pee his pants thinking Ososkie is some kind of Russian spy and wants to lock down the plant and the town."

Bill dug out a cigarette, and lit it. "Then he can break the case and get his ticket punched to D.C. Yeah I know. I still don't see the connection to Nate. Maybe he was trying to shake him down for something, but the fact that they were both killed." Bill shrugged. "What about the other numbers in Nate's address book?"

"Let's see, a bookie out of Portland, a fishing buddy from Kennewick, and a cocktail waitress from Pasco."

Agent Parker stood. "Keep a lid on this, Okay? You need to know with this second homicide the Bureau has its reputation to protect, and it will run over anybody it has to. Do not, I repeat, do not get in the way or you will be taking the train to Leavenworth, clear?"

Bill stood, flicked his cigarette toward the river. "Absolutely."

That afternoon was the memorial service for Nate. All off duty patrolmen were there, looking sharp and solemn in gray uniforms. A few others, Aggie in the front pew, in a black dress and veil, head bowed as the funeral mass was heard. Afterward Bill made his way out and was trying to catch up with Aggie when he was stopped by Father Ryan. Bill shook his hand but Father Ryan did not let it go. A large man in his early 40's, he had started with the Manhattan Project in 43, his first mass in an Army tent. His sparse hair was slicked back, his skin pink with the summer sun and heat. He leaned in close, "Officer Rosen, I understand that I will be saying mass for another of my parishioners."

Bill pulled back, "You're not supposed to know..."

Father Ryan just stepped closer, "I can keep confidences, you need to find out who is doing this."

Bill broke away from the priest and made his way to Aggie. She was standing in a small group of people, co-workers by the look of them. When she saw him she took his hand and squeezed, hard. A sob catching in her throat she said, "Thanks for being here, Bill, call me tonight." Then she broke away and pressed a handkerchief to her eyes and turned back to the group she was with.

Back at Patrol headquarters things were quiet. A brown paper shopping bag was filled with Nate's belongings, all collected from his locker at the station. All of it had been gone through by the FBI. There was not much, a lunch bucket, thermos, a pair of old boots, a spare uniform shirt. A sheet of paper noted that his badge, weapon and, "Other items on his person," were retained for the ongoing investigation.

Chapter Nine

It was after 9:00 by the time Bill made it to Aggie's house. The night was warm. Driving through the neighborhood Bill could hear the sounds of kids playing, a large group running after each other, squeals of laughter and delight in being out in the summer night. From other houses, doors and windows open to catch the breeze, you could see the flickering gray light of a television set. Everywhere there was a sense of bright young families with a bright young future in this bright young town.

Aggie's house was dark except for a light in the kitchen. Behind her house the gentle slope down to the Columbia was lit by an almost full moon rising over the far bank. Bill got out of his truck and walked up to the door, the paper sack under his arm. It was open and he could see Aggie on the couch, head on a pillow, feet tucked under her.

"Hey," Bill said, low and gentle, "I brought some of Nate's stuff."

She stirred, stretched, "Thanks for coming, I just nodded off." Bill could see the change in her face as she came fully awake, the lines of grief returned that had left her as she slept. He remembered when his mother died, how you would fool yourself sometimes when you slept, bring yourself back to a prior time, a happier time, before the death.

She sat up, started to get up, shook her head and then stood. She turned and moved toward the kitchen, "Are you hungry? Everybody was so nice, they brought food, I won't need to shop for a week."

He let her pour him a cup of coffee. They took it and sat out on her back porch, listening to the sounds of the night. Bill lit a cigarette, offered her one and lit hers, reminding him of the Starlite. The moon was up, it's twin reflection distorted in the flow of the river. Bill could see her face concentrating by the glow of her cigarette.

"This is really horrible to say, but all this comes at a bad time. But that was Nate I guess, He always came first. Bill..." She took a drag off her cigarette, sat with her head resting on the chaise lounge, eyes closed. She stayed that way for a moment, and Bill thought she might have given in to the exhaustion he could still read on her face. Then she spoke, in a low voice, almost business like, "There are a few things I should tell you, some of which you may not like, but I just can't get it out of my head that I may be related to Nate's death. Things have gotten..." She shook her head, "Do you know what the new push is all about?"

"You know I'm not paid to think about those things."

She continued in a low steady voice, "I'm working deuterium and tritium production schedules now. Kind of a long way from physics, but I know what it is about and it scares me."

"If it is a safety issue..."

"No, not a safety issue, not for me personally, this is a very safe place to work, you know that. No, it is the discussions about enhanced yield, so many kilotons versus so many megatons, all of it talked about like farmers planting wheat. I feel like I did back in Los Alamos during the war, people getting so caught up in the science of the thing, the god damned beauty of the math." Her voice getting stronger, "And then wrap it up with stars and stripes and say we're just trying to keep the Reds on their side of the wall." She was shaking and sitting forward now, staring out at the river.

She gave him a bleak smile, "I'm sorry Bill, I really am. You don't need to see me like this." She stubbed out the cigarette, stabbing it into the ashtray. "Anyway I am being considered for a transfer, very classified, I will be gone for I don't know how long. To the Pacific. You ever hear of the Mike Shot? Alarm Clock? Super?"

"Hon, like I said...."

"I know, but you know we've been working on the next step."

The last two words sounded like they were in quotes. He did know what she was talking about, at least in snatches. Like a lot of things at Hanford, he knew and didn't know. Production had been gearing up over the past year. Plutonium production had increased, far beyond what would be needed for a few more A-bombs like they dropped on the Japanese. The talk, highly discouraged was that there was going to be a new bomb, a new kind of bomb that would leap ahead of anything the Russians had. Hanford, with the infrastructure in place, was making its deadliest components.

"What does this have to do with Nate?"

"I'm getting to that. I worked directly with Oppenheimer. Brilliant, troubled, he too saw what was happening around him, had the respect of the whole team. When it came close, he actually stepped back and tried to place a moral judgment on what we were doing."

She stopped. A little of the quiet of the night came back. Bill was sitting in a folding chair next to her, a small patio table between them. The dark under the ease of the roof cast them both in shadow. Bill flipped his cigarette out onto the lawn, the tip trailing sparks.

"Without the bombs I would have been dead on a Jap beach."

"I know, I, that's not what I mean. I just mean that like then, we are way ahead of ourselves. We have the ability to do things, make things that have never been made and all we can think to do with it is blow up cities. I'm sorry, this is not what I mean." She stopped.

Bill felt like a jackass. "Hey, don't listen to me. You said there might be something else?"

She went on, "Here's the thing, Nate got hooked up with this guy, Hank or something. Anyway, after a while Nate seemed to have more money. He quit coming around for a loan and even paid me back a little. We even went out once, me, Nate and Hank, although I begged off early. In the last few days before, before he was shot he was, I don't know, distracted. And you know Nate was never like that. Something was going on."

She rocked her head side to side slowly. "I guess I knew Nate would come to a bad end. God, I hate myself for saying that."

Bill stood, walked to the edge of the patio, hands in his pockets, staring out over the river, "You're wrong about Nate. He was a class A screwup in seven different ways but he didn't deserve what happened to him. There's something else going on. Maybe it's like you said, he got into something too deep too fast."

Later, Aggie walked him to his truck. His last view of Aggie, as she turned and walked back to the quiet house, was of a tired woman, frail, shoulders slumped, head down.

Bill drove through the stone quiet town, swing shift had ended, and the graveyard buses had taken their workers out to the plant. In the night the spindly trees and cookie cutter houses were softened, relieved of the harsh glare of the desert sun. Bill passed a patrolman coming from the other direction, driving slowly through the deserted neighborhoods.

The next morning, back downtown before heading out to the Areas he got a call from Agent Parker. "Let's take a walk."

It was sunny but still cool. Parker was in his shirtsleeves as they walked north along Williams. Parker spoke, declining an offered cigarette, "We found the gun. Lady calls in around 7:00 last night in hysterics, apparently one of her sons found the piece next to Ososkie and took it home. Talked his sister into putting an apple on her head, William Tell style. Was surprised as hell when the gun went off."

"Jesus. What happened?"

"Blew the apple off her head, put a little hole in the wall behind her. Who knows, the kid might have a future in law enforcement."

"What about the piece?"

"Don't know yet, 9mm, piece of crap, same as the one that killed Nate. Looks like a match, we won't know for a week or so."

"So that's it? Nate was maybe strong arming this guy and then Ososkie shoots Nate and then feels remorse and walks out to the shelter belt and shoots himself?"

"Maybe."

"Awful neat. What about the rest of your shop."

Parker stopped, "Look, we got our plates full just running background checks on the new hires."

"What about Jennings and Dowd?"

Parker watched a station wagon full of teenagers pulling a boat heading toward the river, "Jennings is smart, but doesn't really have a sense of this place. Dowd can't decide which is better for his career, wrapping up a murder suicide quickly, or still trying to make it about fighting Reds and winning the Cold War."

"What was Osokie's first name?"

"Josef, why"

"Did he have a nick name? Like Hank?"

Parker stopped, thought, "No I'm sure we would have noted it in the file. Try the Manolo's next door to Ososkie. Why, what have you got?"

"Nothing really, just a small detail. Heard Nate was buddies with a guy named Hank. Thought maybe that was Ososkie."

They were back in the lot between the Hanford Patrol Headquarters and the FBI buildings. They heard the swamp coolers come on in one of the buildings, the day was heating up.

Chapter Ten

The Manolos were a bust. The wife could not stop crying and the man was bewildered. Ososkie was a good neighbor, very quiet, went to church and all that. The Feds had searched Ososkie's side of the duplex and carried out anything of interest. The guy was a blank. More and more, Bill could not imagine a sequence of events that allowed Ososkie to get involved with Nate, somehow manage to lure him to the edge of a cooling pond, get the drop on him, shoot him and then take his own life. That just didn't add up.

Bill was back in his office by 10:00. Before he sat Selma came in and handed him a message that said he was to report across the lot to the FBI office. He thought about ignoring it but Selma said that it was urgent. He looked at her and she looked like she was about to cry. "What is it, hon? You look like someone ran over your dog."

She looked away and then back. "I think you're in trouble. It's not my place but you need to be careful. I know you and Nate were friends, so..."

Bill put both hands flat on the desk, "Thanks Selma, I think I can take care of myself. As long as everyone does their job, we'll be okay. Anything else?"

Selma shook her head quickly and went back to her desk. As Bill walked past her on the way out she smiled in a brave face kind of way.

He knew something was up when he came through the door. An agent on the front desk was on duty, a young guy in a sharp suit, he said, "Please remain here and an agent will escort you to the meeting."

Another agent came and they went down the short hallway past the bullpen and into a small conference room. The head of the Hanford Patrol, plus the superintendent of the plant plus six or seven agents were crowded into the small room. Some he recognized, some he did not. Agent Jennings was there looking uncomfortable, Parker was standing at the back and Dowd was up front, a smug expression on his face. The room was hot and close, the windows open, the metal venetian blinds clinking softly as a floor fan stirred the air. Outside the summer sun had claimed the day; hot, flat, white light bounced off the parking lot. Inside no one said anything for a moment. Finally the patrol commander, a man Bill had known for five years read from a typed sheet. "Officer Rosen, you are hereby ordered to surrender your badge and firearm and are suspended from further duties related to the Hanford Site Patrol. Your current clearance level is hereby suspended pending the outcome of an investigation into incidents related to the National Security Act, National Secrets Act and obstruction of a federal investigation related to the Hanford Engineering Works."

Bill was stunned. A part of his mind said, 'careful'. What he said was, "Howard, what the Sam hell is going on?"

The Patrol Commander, graying hair slicked back, looked up from the paper he was reading, angry, "Dammit Bill, you stuck your neck out and it is about to get chopped off, don't make it worse."

Bill removed his sidearm and badge and placed them on the table. He turned to go and Dowd called out, "Where do you think you're going, hotshot?"

They took him into another room, sat him down and for the next four hours had him repeat everything that had happened since Nate's death. He was determined to keep Agent Parker out of it and managed to skirt around any time they had talked. He tried to keep Aggie out of it, but they showed him a photo of him coming out of her house. They showed him another photo too. One that shocked him more than anything else. It showed a woman, neatly dressed, sprawled next to what looked like train tracks, blood spattered across her traveling suit, empty eyes staring at the sky. Silky, Connie, had not made the train out of town.

Finally, they let him go. It came down to this; if they wanted to they could pin Nate's murder on Ososkie and pin Ososkie's murder on him. They had him at Nate's and knew he had looked in Nate's book. At one point Dowd leaned in close, "Look we don't care about Ososkie, but what did you find out, that he was a Red?

That a deal between him and Nate went sour and he got shot? Hell, maybe they should pin a medal on you. Just let us in on it."

"Do you listen to yourself Dowd? Do you practice in front of a mirror? I swear to god, if you are the best we've got, we might as well all start learning Russian."

Soon after that he was headed out of town with a final admonishment that Richland as well as the plant was off limits to him pending a final resolution of his case. Bill headed for home.

By 6:00 that evening he was home. He was staring out the window over the kitchen sink thinking that he would need to either tear out the broken barb wire fence that ran along his west boundary or repair it. Without livestock there was no reason for the fence and broken barb wire would tangle up any animal that came along. Tomorrow he would pull the rest of the fence, maybe leave the posts so he knew where his property ended. He heard a pounding at the door. He opened it and saw his neighbor Heinz standing there with a six pack of Olympia. He wore his cut off overalls, and scuffed brown boots. On his head he wore a gray forage cap. "Well, I heard you got in some trouble." He pushed past Bill and made for the back porch, stepping out onto the patio.

Bill had turned and walked out after his neighbor, "Thanks for the beer, how did you know about my case?"

Heinz waved a hand. "People talk. Da Mailman, Jimmy? He told me." Heinz gave Bill a cold can. They both sat down on the picnic table. The shade of the house provided relief from the evening sun.

Bill opened his with the church key he kept on nail outside the door and passed it to Heinz. They sat for a minute, the cold sweaty cans and the beer tasted good. Heinz shook a little salt onto the top of his can and drained half of it in one gulp. The quiet settled over the house, down the back slope to the river, a duck could be heard splashing in the shallows.

"So what happened? Did you kill some guy?" Heinz finished his first beer and opened a second.

"What are you, a reporter for the Herald?" Bill sipped his beer. Bill didn't mind Heinz; much, anyway. He was blunt as a shovel.

"Okay, I'm just saying you got to clear your name." Heinz finished his second and reached for a third.

"Thanks for the advice. Say, do you see any other Germans that live around here? You know, like you, came over after the war?"

"What, you think maybe we go to the VFW like you guys? I don't think we would be welcome, you know what I mean?" Heinz said with a slightly loopy smile.

"Ouch. I just thought." Bill stood, stretched and looked across the river to the flats of sage and scrub.

Heinz' voice was softer, "They aren't all good people, you know. The ones you brought over. Some on them aren't even who you think they are."

Bill turned, "What do you mean? They were all cleared and double checked."

Heinz shook his head, sat his beer down, leaned forward and placed his forearms on his knees. Bill could see his faded Afrika Korps tattoo on his bicep. Heinz had been captured early in the war and shipped to Toppenish to sit out the war in a POW camp. "Okay, first I'm just taking to you, not those FBI kids, okay?

Bill nodded, intrigued as to where this was going.

"Well there are quite a few of us that came back after the war. You know, the POW's. I got a cousin in Colorado, he was captured in Sicily, worked a sugar beet farm the rest of the war. Did the same thing I did, got back as quick as he could. Now he's got his own business. But see we were just ... you know, dogfaces."

He reached into his overalls and pulled out a short pipe and a bent tin of Sir Walter Raleigh. He packed it slowly and lit it with a wooden match. "I tell you something," he said pointing the pipe at Bill, "I run into a couple who work here, try to say they are from Vienna or some such nonsense. Some of these guys, scientists or not, are as slippery as a bunch of damn eels."

"What do you mean?"

"Me? Maybe I don't know nothing, But I know these guys went from university, to party jobs to munitions plants and back all the time. The real neutral ones? Or the ones that opposed the

Party, they either got out early or were killed. The ones that stayed, they would have kissed Hitler's ass and told him it smelled like roses. Now to hear them tell it not a one even knew a Nazi, much less was a party member. You know?"

Chapter Eleven

By 9:00 the next morning Bill had the barbwire from the fence posts removed. A cool front had moved in overnight and left the air clear. From his house he could see across the flats up the sweep of Rattlesnake, brown against the blue dome of the sky. Dust coming up the road let him know he had a visitor. Wiping the last of the grease off his hands he made his way around the front as a new Ford pulled into his drive. Agent Parker got out of the car, neat as always in his summer weight suit. He stood by the door of his car for a moment.

"Can I come in?"

"Sure Ron, let me make some fresh coffee." This was not an official visit. The FBI always traveled in pairs. Plus, after the last meeting, he got the sense Agent Parker was on the outside of this investigation.

Parker came in and sat down. He placed a package wrapped in a cloth on the table as Bill poured out the last of the pot and reloaded the percolator. "You left something behind."

Bill unfolded the cloth. His .45 had been wiped down and shown lightly. "No, you all wanted to disarm me before I had my little chat with Jennings and Dowd. How is Agent Dowd, by the way?"

Parker waved a hand dismissively. "He's a prick as usual. Spent the rest of the day on the phone with D.C., no doubt letting them know how he broke the case."

"What do you mean broke the case?"

"They have evidence of Bourbeau and Ososkie in a conspiracy to pass secure documents to an outside source. Apparently there was a double cross, Ososkie kills Bourbeau and then filled with remorse for betraying his adopted country, shoots himself."

"Bullshit."

Parker shrugged, "The outside source is an informant working for the FBI."

"Bullshit."

"The documents obtained pertain to uranium processing in the Redox and Purex plants and could have substantially aided the soviet effort to build atomic weapons."

"Bullshit."

"This isn't the first time that the Russians have tried to penetrate this plant. Hell, right from the get go they knew about what we were doing here. And since...never mind."

"Since the push for the H-bomb you would expect a stepped up attempt at penetration."

"You did not hear that from me." Parker accepted a mug from Bill, the percolator making burbling noises in the background.

"Christ Ron, I'm not an idiot." Bill fiddled in his kitchen, gathering a sugar bowl and spoons. He did all of this with the efficient, confirmed motions of long practice.

"Anyway, you will be in the clear. Nobody thinks you would have killed Ososkie. Dowd is pushing for an extended suspension to, as he says, double check your background."

"So that's it then. Nate and Ososkie decide to gather up conveniently available documents to sell to the Russians, which were just lying around the Purex plant. Happen to know a spy to sell them to, who happens to be an FBI informant, sell them, and have a meeting outside the K-reactor where Ososkie, who from his file looks like a ninety pound weakling, gets the drop on Nate, shoots him and dumps him in the pond. Later, but not too much later, feels despondent, wanders out to the shelter belt and shoots himself."

"Something like that." Parker said with a neutral, FBI copyrighted bland expression on his face.

"Bullshit." This time Bill did not put much emphasis into his response, resigned to the story.

"We found documents at Ososkie's place. Classified, hidden or at least concealed."

"Really? Who found them?"

Parker looked uncomfortable. "Dowd."

"Dowd or Jennings and Dowd?"

"Just Dowd. Jennings was with the body. Agent Dowd responded to the residence with a couple of officers from Richland."

"Who?"

"Come on Bill, I'm out on a limb here. I'm filling you in because I know that you are not going to let this go. On the other hand, everybody wants this to go away."

"It stinks Ron. Who killed Connie?"

"Unrelated. A robbery gone bad. East Pasco." He shrugged again, as if saying, you know how it is.

"What about Aggie?"

"That's yet to be determined. As yet there is nothing to tie her to Nate and Ososkie. On the other hand she is cleared at the highest level. Plus she has been seeing you."

"So if I play ball she is in the clear?" Bill filled both their cups.

"Something like that." Agent Parker stirred sugar into his.

"Is that why you came out here."

"That, plus the coffee."

Bill stood and leaned back against the kitchen sink, facing Parker. He looked at Parker and then nodded, "Thanks for the update, Ron. Here's what I think. I think you were sent out here to deliver a message that if I want to keep my job, help Aggie keep hers, and continue on my merry way, I need to pretend that all of this is over. Everybody comes out smelling like a rose except for me, and on balance there is nothing more than a letter in my file and little shit on my boots. But you did more than that Ron, you gave me a few more details than necessary and you know I won't just let it sit."

Parker raised his cup, "I have no idea what you are talking about. But I do love your coffee." He still had his regulation bland face, but his eyes nodded.

"So what is happening with the Bureau these days?" Bill sat down.

Agent Parker stretched out his legs. "You are right about a couple of things. There is a change and I don't know if I like it. I joined the Bureau in '44, right out of law school. The war had changed what we did, mostly for the better. We weren't chasing bootleggers and two bit bank robbers anymore; we were doing important work for the war effort. Like what we were doing here. Some of the agents from the old days couldn't hack it, didn't understand that spying and sabotage were not just publicity opportunities for J. Edgar. But those of us that came in during the war, we knew, at least we thought we did, what we were up against. Did you know that not only did we find the Germans and Japanese spying on us, but the Russians and the British too? The Germans though, they were good. Dedicated, even more than the Russians. They of course had the communist party plus sleepers, but we had been developing our sources inside that bunch of losers for a long time. I remember interviewing a German spy in 45, right before the war ended in Europe. He had the best cover I had ever seen, right down to the Kansas accent. Was working at an aircraft plant."

"How did you catch him?"

"His papers. They were too good. I mean they were fine but he had a birth certificate, an old dusty thing from a little town in west Kansas. Trouble was the courthouse had burned down and all the records were destroyed. Anyway he was still trying to sabotage war production even though Germany had lost the war."

Parker stood, "I need to get back. Thanks for the coffee. You'll be getting a call, you're off till Monday." He picked up his hat, "Be careful with that thing, the trigger pull is very light."

"So you're telling me how to maintain my equipment now?"

Agent Parker shook his head as he went out the door, "Cowboys."

The dust settled slowly as Parker's car retreated down the dirt lane and onto the highway.

Later that day Bill saw another dust trail approaching his house. Two visitors in one day, he thought maybe he should clean up more.

Frank Richardson stepped out of the car. Out of uniform, he looked younger than his 22 two years. He wore a short sleeved sport shirt tucked into tan pants. The day was heating up and he already looked hot. He walked up the drive and Bill noticed he had the stride of a natural athlete.

"Frank, what brings you all the way out here?"

"Hello Lieutenant..."

"Call me Bill, damn it, we're off the clock. Besides I am not sure of my rank or job status."

"No, no the word is you will be back Monday."

"Word is, huh?"

Frank blushed. "Yeah, I know I used to chew out the fellas for talking too much, but a lot has happened since you were suspended."

"Like what?"

Frank leaned against his car, started ticking points off with his fingers, "First there was a meeting with the whole patrol, stating that the case was closed, it had been an intentional death, it was investigated by the FBI and that security had not been breached although issues of national security were involved. We were all instructed not to speculate, just do our jobs. You know the rest, safety and security is job one."

"So how did you feel about that?" Bill held open the screen door to let Frank in. They came into the open living room. The concrete floor still held some of the morning's cool. Frank sat on the couch, Bill settled into his old chair, both bought surplus from the project.

Frank stopped and thought about it. "Okay I guess. It's the same kind of chicken shit we got in the MP's; I just didn't think there would be as much of it here. I guess I thought, you know, it'd be different."

"You like it here, don't you?"

"Yeah, it's a good place. Richland will be a great place to raise a family, good schools, everything new and all. Like the rest of the country, maybe better. Don't you?"

"What?" Bill lit a cigarette.

"Like it here?" Frank crossed his leg, looking around, taking in the house.

"For me it's a little complicated. You know that school they just finished on Van Giesen? Jason Lee? You know behind it where the air raid siren tower is with all those dead trees in the field around it?"

"What about it?"

"It's nothing, right? Just a bunch of dead trees between the end of the last streets heading north to the barricade."

"So?"

"See, that's the thing. To me I don't see it that way. I see the peach and apricot trees the way they used to be. There were more than 200 of them, and Torvald Mortensen, he was this big dumb bastard that owned the orchards. My grandfather built the canals that brought the water to his orchards. It was way the hell out of Richland, the old Richland. I used to ride out there from Hanford, the town of Hanford; my dad had me as a ditch rider from the Spring on. Those were great peaches. We shipped them all over the country."

Bill waved his hand, blew out smoke, "Anyway, it's not that things have changed, it's that everything was scraped off and then everyone is pretending nothing was ever here. And pretending is not a good habit to get into. Once you start, it's hard to stop."

"You mean like with Nate."

"Exactly like with Nate."

Chapter Twelve

Aggie came out at 4:30 that afternoon. Bill was out front shoveling the last of a load of gravel out of his pickup into the circular drive in front of his house. He had started after Frank left. The long afternoon had turned cooler. A light breeze was keeping the flies and mosquitoes down to a minimum. He was shirtless, wearing an old pair of dungarees, work boots and a straw cattleman with a broken brim. Again he saw the dust coming down his driveway. He thought it might be Heinz but could just see the end of Heinz's old Nash in his driveway. Also whoever it was, they were moving at a pretty good clip. Soon Aggie's Chevy pulled into his drive. She stopped and the fine dust that had been following her slipped up around the car, drifting forward to envelope them both. Bill leaned the shovel against the house and picked up his t-shirt, wiping his face. She sat in the car for a minute, hands on the wheel, staring at him. She was wearing a scarf over her head and large sunglasses. The thought flitted through his head that she looked like a movie star. He took off his hat and pulled the shirt on over his head. The dust settled and so did the quiet.

"Hello Aggie, you should have called, I would have cleaned myself up, although you wouldn't believe the company I've had today." He walked over to open her door. She stepped out and walked ahead of him to the door. He slipped past her and opened the screen.

She still had not said anything to him. Finally she turned and said, "We need to talk, but I'm so damn mad at you I could spit." With that she stalked into the house.

He followed her in. He wanted to say, 'What the hell did I do?' Instead he said, "So, what's on your mind?"

She turned on him, "Did you know about the wiretap on my phone? The photos? The photos of me and you at my house? My brother is murdered and they are treating me like a, like a criminal, a suspect? Tell me you didn't know any of this."

"Who told you?"

"Answer my question first. Did you know this was going on?"

"Well, I figured they would. Look I didn't have anything to do with it. It's the FBI. You should have known they were going to push this for all it was worth."

"Should have known? Christ Bill, what's next? Are they going to bug my house? See if I have a secret Russian lover? What the hell is going on?"

He held both hands up, put one gently on her elbow and guided her to the kitchen table. She sat, took off her sunglasses and set them on the Formica table with a clack. Rubbed her eyes and started to undo her driving scarf.

Bill sat across from her, "Start from the beginning. Who told you?"

"It was two of them, a disgusting little fat man and a quiet one. They came to my house last night, around 6:00. I don't remember, I was probably asleep on the couch." She looked at him and briefly smiled, "Like the other night when you came by. They came in flashing their badges and started off polite. Said they did not want to bother me at work. How important I was to the project and all that. Then they started in on Nate, on how they had the goods. They actually said that, 'we've got the goods on him'. It was awful."

"Jennings and Dowd."

"What?"

"The FBI. Agents Jennings and Dowd, right?"

"I think so. Bill, what's really going on, tell me, please" Aggie reached across the table and grabbed his hands. He could see she was rattled, the loss of her brother and now this.

"Okay, here goes. I've been poking around. The Feds don't like it and actually gave me a pretty clear warning that, well never mind. I aim to keep digging. Hell, everybody on the force expects me to. I've got a few things I want to check out, but the whole story about Nate and Ososkie and passing secrets is as phony as a three dollar bill." He stopped, not knowing exactly how far he wanted to let Aggie in, how much to keep from her.

She looked at him, picking up her sunglasses and tapping them on the table. "You know more don't you?"

"Tell me about his friends. Who were those two jokers in that Ford the other night? Could it have been Ososkie?"

Aggie got up and wandered into the living room, stood looking out the French doors down the slope to the river. The sun was lowering to the west, casting long shadows off Rattlesnake Mountain. She turned toward Bill, "Not Ososkie. At least I don't think so. I don't know, maybe I'd seen them before, I'm not sure. If Nate was slippery with you, he was twice as slippery with me. You have a sister?"

"No, just a brother. We're not that close."

"Well, we were. At least as close as Nate got to anybody. Still."

"Still what?"

"I bet you saw it too. Liked to come off as a big simple guy, not a thing going on. Then you'd find out he'd set up a betting pool on the World Series. You know, it was like he had different parts of his life going on at the same time, but could never put them all together."

"I know what you mean. He was smart, real smart, but he used those smarts to do just enough to get by. He was lazy that way." Bill lit a cigarette, offered her one. She shook her head.

"No, I don't think so. I mean yes, he always tried to get out of work. I did most of his chores on the ranch just to keep the peace in the house. He and our father, well, you should have seen the way they went round and round. He left when he was 17, quit in his senior year in high school, lit out for Seattle I guess, we were never sure. I was in college, making my own escape. He came to my graduation. My folks couldn't make the trip; mother was sick and father, they had lost the ranch and were living in town." She stared ahead, Bill could see her face tighten, knew the tears would come but wanted to hold off a little.

"He came for me, his big sister. That was '40. I was so lonely Bill, you just don't know. I liked Stanford; they had already given me a scholarship for graduate school. The people, the students and professors, were all real sweet. But when Nate showed up, he had his uniform on, he had just completed basic training, it was like, it was like we had both graduated, you know? We had made it out of a dead end and the future was open."

"Did you see him much? I mean before he went overseas?"

She shook her head slowly, "No, just that one time. I got some post cards. He was down in Fort Lenard Wood. Then he went overseas. Our folks died within a year of each other during the war. I made the arrangements and took care of it all."

By now the sun was behind the hills to the west. Long, high pink clouds stippled the sky. Aggie was silent, relaxed, or at least still. Bill sat, not knowing what to do, settled for patting her hand, just that. She held his and squeezed. He could feel the trembling. She squeezed harder, her red nails digging into his hard palm. And then it passed, she relaxed, took a handkerchief out of her bag, dabbed at her face. "Thanks for listening. I guess I just needed to go on a bit."

"Let's go eat. There's a joint out here I bet you haven't been to. What do you say?"

"Sure, but let me buy for bending your ear."

"Not a chance, sweetheart. I need to shower. Fifteen minutes. Tops."

The restaurant was on the highway, just before the turn off to Benton City; run by a large Mexican family Bill had known forever. When they came in Aggie immediately began speaking Spanish to the proprietor and by the time they had sat down she was being treated like a long lost daughter.

"Where'd you pick up Spanish?"

She shrugged, "College, but I was at Los Alamos, remember? Used it there. Loved the area around the site."

They were interrupted by the waitress bringing large plates of food. Bill thanked the waitress.

"You're polite."

"You seem surprised."

"I mean yeah, you're nice enough. I mean to the waitress. You did it the other night. You always say thank you or whatever to the people who wait on you." She had a kind of a half sly smile.

Bill looked embarrassed and dug into the food. "Whoa, what is this? It's good, but I don't think it's on the regular menu."

"Chicken Mole. Good, huh?"

"Real good. I need to bring you here all the time."

She blew on a bite of chicken. "Don't get ahead of yourself."

Later, back at his place, they had drinks and sat outside, talking about nothing. The quiet settled in, and they sat in the dark, listening to the river below, seeing its long gray shadow. Across the river on the flats of the reservation a car's headlights briefly shown moving down the service road.

"When are you leaving?" He said.

"Soon, maybe the end of the week. The team will meet in Los Alamos for briefings and then we go from there." Her voice was soft, detached.

"Where?"

"It's not a good idea, with all the..." she waived her hand dismissively.

"You're not coming back, are you?"

She turned toward him. He reached over and pushed her hair back around her ear. "I don't blame you, kid. You got more on the ball than is needed around here."

She said nothing for a moment. "I should go." She got up and moved through the French doors into the living room. He got up and reached for his cigarettes, stood and followed her. He switched on a light, feeling awkward, glad she had come, not wanting her to go, not knowing what to do about it. She turned to him, hugging him, her hair tickling his neck. They stood that way for a moment and then she moved back, just out of his arms, "Bill I..."

At that moment there was a slight 'tink' from one of the panes of glass in the door and Aggie was thrown back, red blood appearing on her chest. Bill then heard the gunshot, automatically estimating that it had come from across the river. He spun and reached for Aggie and felt a white hot pain across his back, the force of it pushing him down on his knees. Gritting his teeth against the pain he grabbed Aggie, dragging her back from the shattered glass door as another bullet crashed through the glass, gouged a hole in the concrete floor and caromed into the room. Bill, again, was unconsciously listening for the sound of the shot, hearing it come later. A thousand yards? Less?

Stooping over Aggie he could see her breathing, her eyes staring around wildly and her mouth trying to make words. He scooted over to the open kitchen, switched off the light, reached under the sink and pulled out a flashlight and first aid kit. He scooted back to Aggie and grabbed a blanket off the couch, threw it over both of them to shield the light and turned on the flashlight. In the close space she lit up like a spotlight, he could see the blood pouring out of a wound in her chest, bubbling slightly. She was in shock, her pale skin looking even more transparent, the color draining from her face, her lips paling to blue. Working fast, not knowing if the shooter was on his way to finish the job, Bill turned off the light, threw back the blanket and ripped the bottom of her light dress. He put and kept pressure on the wound and applied a bandage from the kit, winding the dressing with her torn dress. She was starting to come around, moaning, clearly in shock.

Bill thought quickly, the shooter had to be across the river, with no easy way across. The Horn Rapids Bridge was at least a mile away west and the other bridge to Richland the same distance. He gathered Aggie up and headed for the front door. As he lifted her the pain in his back hit him like a sledgehammer. He could feel his shirt soaking with his own blood. He came through the door and got to his truck in the driveway. The keys were in it and he slid Aggie in and propped her beside him, starting the truck and gunning it toward town. He fishtailed it on the dirt road, stayed out of the ditch by inches and got up on the highway, standing on the accelerator. The bridge over the Yakima flashed by, and he looked up the road, unable to see headlights. The road was empty and passed in a blur all the way to the guard station at the edge of town. He slowed, suddenly woozy from the ride and the returning pain in his back. He recognized the man in the gate house, and yelled to him, Mitch, I'm heading to Kadlec, call ahead and tell them Aggie's been shot."

The Patrolman flashed his light inside the cab of the truck, saw blood covering Bill and blood seeping from Aggie's wound, stepped back, "Shit Slim, you think you can make it across town?"

Bill gunned the engine and roared off. After half a block, he saw flashing lights in his rear view mirror and heard the sound of sirens. The town, dead quiet this time of night, allowed for a quick run to the hospital. By the time he pulled into the parking lot in front of the doors with the lighted Red Cross over them, he was starting to drift off. He turned off the engine and started to lift Aggie, when both doors of the truck were opened and he and Aggie were lifted out by burly orderlies. He started to protest but his legs gave out and he allowed them to put him on a gurney. The last thing he saw was two orderlies and two nurses rapidly pushing Aggie through the double doors into the hospital. He started to lay back when the pain hit again, this time graying out his vision. The last thing he heard was, "On his side, on his side, his back is torn open."

Chapter Thirteen

Sunlight streamed in through the open window. A fan oscillated back and forth stirring the warm air. Bill blinked and looked around. He didn't recognize the room or bed he was in. Oh, yeah, he thought, I got shot.

"Good thing you know how to duck." Bill was startled to see a large man in cowboy boots and a Benton County Sheriff's uniform and holding a Stetson sitting in the corner. There seemed to be a small space between Bill and his thoughts. Sheriff Carson.

"Sheriff..."

"Easy Bill, you have been out since they sewed you up."

"Sheriff?"

"Aggie's still touch and go. Through and through, broke a rib, punctured a lung, lost a lot of blood, you saved her getting her here."

Bill felt himself getting sleepy. The next time he woke he had a pounding headache and a terrible thirst. There was a glass of water with a straw on the night stand. He started to reach for it and pain snaked across his back. Just then a nurse in starched whites came into the room saw what he was doing and pushed his hand back.

"Let me do that. Lie still or you'll pop the stitches." She reached over and cranked the bed so he was sitting up. She then handed him a pill and gave him the glass.

"What's this?"

"Penicillin. Keep your wound from getting infected." She looked at him through steel framed glasses. She had salt and pepper hair cut short under her cap. "You lost a lot of blood, surprised you were able to drive."

"How do you know about last night?

"I was one of the people that pulled you and your wife out of your truck."

"How is she?"

"She's still critical, but it looks good." Thank god, Bill thought.

"Can I see her?"

"Nope. The doc will be by and let you know what you can do. You up for a visitor? I got several outside. I'll let the ones with guns in last."

A moment later the door opened and Bill's father came in. Hat in hand he looked drawn and tired. He stood over the bed; slightly stoop shouldered and a slight smile on his face.

"Well son, how you doing?"

"I guess not so good. Can you tell me anything about what happened?"

"I didn't hear much, Buddy told me you and Aggie had been shot and you drove here. They told him it was some kind of accident. Now he is madder than hell, because there are all these FBI folks out there. They're talking jurisdiction, and you know how Buddy feels about that."

Buddy Carson, Benton County Sheriff, had an uneasy relationship with everything to do with Hanford. He had been Sheriff of Benton County since before the Manhattan Project. He had seen the old towns disappear, the plant and the new town built, and himself ignored by the federal government. The sheriff's office was in Prosser, up the Yakima Valley from

Richland. He had known Bill's father and their family for years, welcomed Bill's father to Prosser and helped him get established after he had been turned out of his home during the war. Buddy lost two sons during the war, and had greeted Bill warmly when he had returned.

At that moment they heard shouting in the hall outside his room. Buddy Carson came in, followed by agents Jennings and Dowd, followed by the nurse. They were continuing the conversation they had been having outside, in the strained tones of men who want to shout but who are constrained to keep their voices lowered.

"God damn it to hell and back. You cannot have it both ways. You cannot tell me that this is Hanford business when it happened in the county and then say that it is a closed case. I don't give a shit what you tell yourself but this was attempted murder, not some kind of accident."

Dowd pushed up to Sheriff Carson, expecting the big man to step back. Carson stood his ground putting them nose to nose, or nose to chin given Dowd's shorter stature. "Now look here, ah, Sheriff, you do not understand the ramifications of a case like this. It needs to be handled in the interests of national security; we wouldn't want wild speculation in the press to jeopardize an ongoing investigation."

"Nobody is going to say anything to the 'press', if by that you mean the Tri-City Herald. I've been doing this job long enough to know bullshit when I hear it. So unless you get a formal injunction I am going to find out who did this and prosecute them to the full extent of the law."

Dowd turned to Jennings. "I've had just about enough of Matt Dillon here. I'm going back to the office and start the paperwork to shut him up."

He turned back around and started to shoulder around Sheriff Carson who stepped out of the way. When he was past, Carson reached out one hand and tapped him on the shoulder hard enough to leave dents in is suit. "Maybe your tough guy act works back east, but out here never mistake courtesy for cooperation."

Carson turned back to Jennings who stood with his hands up, a gesture Bill was becoming familiar with. "Okay Jennings, are you going to be an asshole like your partner or can we talk to Bill here together. Pardon me, Mary." He nodded in the direction of the nurse.

At this opening she stepped in. "This is quite the manly show but you all have another 10 minutes tops before I throw you out. The patient needs rest." She glared at the three men standing around the bed. She turned and left.

Bill's father looked at the two law men. "I don't know what's going on here; all I care about is Bill and Aggie. You two need to stop pissing on each other's legs and figure out who did this. Bill, help them out and don't go all muley, you know at least Buddy will do the right thing." With that he nodded at the two others and left the room.

Sheriff Carson, chastened, pulled up a chair and sat down. Jennings stood on the other side of the bed. Jennings said to Bill, "Thanks, Bill, for your cooperation. I will personally keep Sheriff Carson here in the know about the investigation. My partner, Agent Dowd, can be a bit abrasive at times."

At this Sheriff Carson snorted, "Yeah, and I tend to rise to the bait. So tell us what do you think happened?'

Bill had been watching everything. He felt tired. He felt himself going in and out; awake but not really part of what was going on. Now Sheriff Carson and Agent Jennings were looking at him, and there was something really important he wanted to say. Nope, there it went.

The nurse came in. "Out."

Bill woke again in the middle of the night. His back was sore; he could feel the stitches pull when he shifted his weight. From past experience he knew that he was starting to heal. His head felt clearer than before but he had trouble remembering everything that had happened. He remembered Carson and Dowd squaring off, did that really happen? He remembered the nurse, Mary, ordering them around like so many children. Aggie, he needed to see Aggie.

Slowly he sat up and swung his legs over the edge of the bed. The room rocked a bit and then settled down. Good start he thought. He was attached to a drip bag hanging on a stand. A few minutes fiddling and he removed the needle in his arm. Feet on the cold tile, hanging on to the end of the bed, he stood. He shuffled to the small bathroom, stood over the toilet and took a long grateful piss. He looked at himself in the mirror. He looked haggard but OK. When he was done he turned around and looked over his shoulder. All he could see was a long diagonal bandage. He pulled part of it off and he could just see part of the wound that ran diagonally across his back. An ugly red channel crisscrossed with black stitches. He could feel it, going from just above his right hip across and exiting just under his left shoulder blade. The bullet had lacerated the meat of his back, but had not hit bone. For just a second he thought of one of his men, Fletcher? Who had been with him in the Pacific? They were in Manila and been pinned down. Fletcher had caught one in the back, severed his spine. As he lay dying he had told Bill not to let his mother know he had been shot in the back. He didn't want her to think he had been running away.

He shuffled to the small closet. His dad had brought him a pair of dungarees and plaid shirt. He had also brought him a change of underwear and an old pair of cowboy boots. Good enough, thought Bill. He sat on the bed, pulled the hospital gown off over his head and began the slow process of putting on his clothes. He had his pants on when a nurse came in. She looked startled.

"What do you think you are doing?"

"Getting dressed." Bill was glad to see that it was not Mary. This nurse was much younger and less sure of her authority.

"You have to get back in bed. You are not scheduled for discharge for another three days."

"I'm leaving tonight."

"You can't."

Bill finished pulling on his socks and slipped into his boots. "Honey, hand me that shirt. Could you give me a hand with it?"

She held it as he slipped his arms through the sleeves. He buttoned it but left it untucked. He sat again on the edge of the bed. He was sweating and exhausted. The nurse stared at him. "You can't just leave; there is no one to discharge you."

"I'll just discharge myself. Tell you what, bring me a smoke and a form to sign and I'll sign it."

She came back a few minutes later with the head nurse and a clipboard. The head nurse looked at him, gave him the clipboard and left. The nurse pulled out a pack of Tarrytons and gave him one, lighting one herself. She sat and looked at him while he read and signed the forms. The hospital was quiet; a janitor pushed a cart along the hall outside. "I've been here the last two nights, you're not ready to go home, you know that, right?"

"You're Charlene right? I tell you Char, I don't do well in hospitals. Can you tell me where Aggie Bourbeau is?

"She is still in critical care, the next wing over. Tell you what, wait here, I'll get a wheelchair and take you over. I'm not sure you could make it on your own."

Bill was wheeled down the long hall, around a corner and down another hall. They passed through double doors that said surgery/recovery. Straight ahead was a nurse's station. Across from this were individual rooms. Bill could see a patrolman in front of one room, in a chair, nodding but keeping awake. The area had the feel of relaxed attention. It was night and the lights were dimmed, but the nurses looked alert as they carried trays into the rooms or checked charts. Behind the desk was an older man with a bad comb over and round glasses. He had a white coat with a stethoscope sticking out of one pocket. He looked tired. He looked up from his writing on a chart and said to Bill, "What the hell do you think you are doing. Nurse, get that man back to his room."

"Nice to see you too Doc. Thanks Char, I'll take it from here."

Bill slowly struggled out of the wheelchair. "Doc. I'm leaving and there is not a damn thing you can do about it. I just needed to come by and see my girl."

He made his way to the room with the cop in front of it. "Hi Sam, they got you pulling the night shift, I see."

"Officer, do not let that man in the room." The Doc pointed at Bill.

"I'll just be a minute. If I take too long, have Sam here shoot me."

Sam grinned and opened the door for Bill. "Don't take long Bill, better do what they say."

Bill entered the room and his stomach flip flopped. Aggie was under an oxygen tent, small and pale. She lay on her back, a tube coming out of her side draining into a bottle hanging off the bed filled with dark blood and pus. Another bottle held fluids going into her arm. Under her gown, Bill could see bandages swathed her torso.

Bill went and stood by her bed. He looked at her, willing her to live. Guilt washed over him for putting her in danger. It was a guilt that was slowly turning to anger. After a few minutes he turned and walked out. He patted Sam on the shoulder, "Thanks for being here. You watching her round the clock?"

"You bet, Slim. Roger Fulling will take the shift at 7:00. We'll keep a good eye on her."

The doctor was surprised that he hadn't been listened to. "No visitors mean no visitors, period. Now back to your room. I can keep the FBI out and I can keep you out."

Bill turned to the doctor, "FBI?"

"Agent Jennings has been here three times in the last two days. He's not getting in and neither should you."

Bill waved him off, "Okay doc, you're the boss. You can wheel me back now Char."

Bill sat with care in the wheelchair. The nurse turned him around and they went out through the double doors. He couldn't see her face, but there was a smile in her voice, "Doctor Jameson is not used to having anyone disobey an order. The look on his face is worth the chewing out he will give me later about bringing you here. They made it to the intersection of the halls and Bill stopped the chair and stood up. "Thanks, hon. I got to run."

With that he got up and started for the door. The night intake nurse looked up and said "Hey!" as he walked out into the warm night.

Chapter Fourteen

Every step was pain, but the night air felt great. It was just after 3:00 AM; the town dead silent. He walked out of the hospital toward the middle of town and the 1100 Area. It was just a few blocks and he figured he could make it in one go, or stop and rest if he had to. After just a few minutes, a patrol car slowed down next to him.

The officer leaned out of the car, it was Frank. "Get in Slim, Sam just called from the hospital and said you might need a ride."

"Thanks. Just take me to headquarters; I got a few things to check before I head home." Bill said as he eased into the passenger side of the car, wincing as he rested his back against the seat.

"You look pretty bunged up. Maybe I should take you back to the hospital." Frank said.

"No, Frank. Just take me to headquarters. What the heck are you doing out this late anyway?" Bill said, shifting, trying to find a more comfortable position.

Frank kept his eyes forward, hands at the proper ten and two position. He spoke slowly, in a tone that surprised Bill, "We're all out. We're going to get him. This isn't about you or Nate anymore. This is about all of us."

"Damn it, Frank. Go home will ya? The Feds are on it. They can handle it." Bill said.

Frank glanced at him, "Come on Bill, you don't believe that."

"But that's the way it is, Frank. Go home, kiss your wife, go to bed. Tomorrow come in and do the job. That's how you can help. Okay?"

As he walked in to Patrol Headquarters, the night shift watch commander looked up, "Jesus Slim, you look like hell."

"As far as I know, Jesus did not have anything to do with it. Mind if I take a seat back here?"

There were a number of extra officers around, mostly just standing around having coffee, getting in the way.

"Alright, everybody knows I got shot. I don't know who or why, but everybody who is not on shift needs to clear out. Period." He looked around. There were a few protests but people began to shuffle out.

He grabbed a desk in the bullpen, searched around and pulled out paper and a pencil and began writing a list. He wanted to get things down as quick as possible, knowing he would forget details if he waited. There were a couple things nagging at him that he could not quite capture. Making a list would help. He was convinced that the target at his house was Aggie, and so did everyone else. She was related to Nate, and so somehow constituted a connection to his case. Why shoot her at all was a big question, and why do it from across the river. He knew if you wanted to murder someone, you needed to be close to make sure the job got done. Nate had been taken out that way and so had Ososkie. The next question was what connected the three together. Nate and

Aggie, brother and sister; they did see each other from time to time. She brought him food and probably did his laundry. He took her to dinner, mooched money from her, but what else? She was his sister. She got him a job here or at least put in a good word. What else?

Then there was Nate, perennial screw-up, marginal cop, gambler, but not enough to get him killed. And Ososkie. Straight arrow, refugee who just wanted a quiet life, and thought he had found it out here. The spy stuff just didn't wash; Nate and Ososkie just didn't go together. But if he was a bystander, then what was all the evidence planted in his house about, and why was the FBI so interested in covering it up. It didn't add up. Not right away.

He went back to the watch commander. "Do you know what happened to my truck?"

"Yeah, they brought it over after the FBI went through it. They made some noise about keeping it as part of a crime scene but we ignored them. Maintenance cleaned it out for you. They said they had to use a steam hose to get the blood out."

"Who over at the FBI is on the case?"

"It was Jennings and Dowd, but they got pulled off after they had a run in with Sheriff Carson." He grinned, "They didn't figure on the Federal Court Judge being hunting buddies with the Sheriff. Slapped them down real quick."

"Who has the case now?" Bill said.

"Parker. Seems he is on better terms with Carson."

"Do me a favor. Call over there and leave a message for Parker letting him know I want to see him tomorrow. Tell him to just come out to my place around noon."

"You got it, Bill. I'll have maintenance bring your truck around. You okay to drive?"

"Mostly."

The drive home was hell. He leaned forward to keep his back off the seat and that helped, but every time he shifted gears he could feel the stitches stretch. By the time he bumped along the dirt road to his house he could feel the bandages getting loose and sticky from blood. He came in the door, and without turning on a light went into the bathroom, slowly stripped off his clothes and dry swallowed four aspirin. Naked, he went into his bedroom and carefully lay down.

He woke with a start. The sun was streaming in the window. Someone was changing his bandage. The nurse with the steel framed glasses was just taping up his shoulder. He thought that the hospital looked like his bedroom.

"Hold still. That little stunt last night cost you two or three days healing. Plus you bled all over your sheets. Where are the clean ones?" She said wadding up the blood spotted sheets.

He realized he was naked lying on the bed. He grabbed a blanket that had been knocked to the floor.

"Oh, please. Just lie still. Sheets?" She said.

"Uh, closet off the kitchen, next to the washer." He gently sat up. He could hear her speak to someone in the living room. He lay back and went to sleep.

He woke again. It was later but still morning. The sun was in his face. A clean sheet covered him. He could smell coffee and hear a shh-shh plop coming from the living room. Slowly he stood up, quietly put on a pair of boxer shorts. His gun belt was on a chair. He quietly slipped the .45 out of the holster and slowly pushed the slide back. He stepped into the living room and saw Frank on his hands and knees scrubbing the blood stain off the floor. A scoped 30.06 leaned against the kitchen table. He turned and dropped the rag into the reddish soapy water.

"Hey Bill. Just thought I'd get the stain off the floor if I could." Frank got to his feet and went to the stove. "Want coffee?"

Bill was still getting the cobwebs out of his head. He did notice that Frank had stopped calling him Officer Rosen. "Yeah sure, coffee." He sat down in one of the kitchen chairs. "Isn't this your day off?"

"Yup. Sugar, right?" he placed a mug and the sugar bowl and a spoon in front of Bill.

Bill stirred sugar into the cup. He felt a little awkward in his boxer shorts. Frank had on dungarees cuffed up over work boots and a short sleeved sport shirt. He shook out a cigarette and offered one to Bill.

Bill took one and lit it. His back was very stiff and there was pain but he felt halfway human. "Was the nurse here?"

"Yeah. Came about eight. Said the Doc might come by later. She wasn't happy you left Kadlec." Frank shifted the rifle to lean against the door jamb.

"You here last night?" Bill took a drag on his cigarette.

"Yeah. Followed you home. Thought you might run off the bridge getting here." Frank looked at him.

Bill nodded at the rifle. "You any good with that?"

"Qualified expert marksman." Frank said.

"Good. Might just need that." Bill stood and slowly shuffled back to the bedroom and began putting on clothes. He called from the bedroom, "Can you scramble some eggs? If you're being my maid at least you can make breakfast."

Later that day Bill set up three empty oil cans down the slope of his house. "Let's go for a drive Frank, and bring your rifle."

They made their way across the Horn Rapids Bridge, stopped at the Yakima

Barricade and showed their badges. The guard on duty was surprised to see them. "Hell Slim, I thought you were still in the hospital." The Feds and the Patrol had been over the logs at the gate and found that no one had passed through surrounding the time Bill and Aggie were shot.

They made their way down the access road across the river from Bill's house. They stopped and got out when they could see it; sitting on the rise from the river, the sand and sagebrush giving way to the small grassy lawn behind the house. The back porch and the patio with the two lounge chairs were all clearly visible. The angle from the road did not quite give a full view of the French doors.

"What did the Feds say about the shooting?" Bill stood by the door of Frank's car.

Frank had gotten out and was standing next to Bill, looking across and judging distances. "They said that it probably took place from around here. The shooter was on the reservation, stopped on the road, probably laid the gun on a rest on the hood of the car and shot at you both from that position." Frank held his hand up to shade his eyes, shook his head. He got the rifle out, rummaged around in the back seat and pulled out a blanket. He wadded it up and put it on the hood of his car. He sighted through the scope. He stood that way, hunched over the rifle, braced against the car. Finally, he lifted his head. He looked at Bill, shook his head. "Didn't happen. At least not that way. Come take a look."

Bill eased himself into a shooters position, mindful of his back. He wrapped his arm around the sling and pulled it tight to his shoulder. Looking through the scope he saw the back of his house, the porch and patio. The overhang from the veranda cut off the view of the French doors at knee height. He panned down to find the oil cans. Eight hundred yards easy. The chance of a miss at this distance was too great. Bill straightened up. "Let's go for a walk."

They made their way toward the river. From the access road, the flats sloped down to the Yakima River. They walked along looking right and left, their feet sinking in the soft sandy soil. Nearer the river the land became rocky, black basalt thrusting out of the sand. Halfway between the access road and the river, Bill stopped, next to a boulder and looked across the river, "This is where I would set up. See what you think."

Frank crouched behind the boulder and laid the rifle across the top. He assumed a classic sitting position, elbows on both knees, rifle tucked into his shoulder, eye on the scope. "Yeah, this would do it. You have a clear shot. Slightly above head height looking into your living room. I could knock a coffee cup out of your hand from here."

"What about three times in say, ten seconds?" Bill gazed across the river, even without the scope seeing clearly into his house.

"No. Maybe two shots. But not with a hunting rifle and not at night."

Bill kept staring at the back of his house. "You said you qualified Expert Marksman?"

Frank looked at him, "Yeah. Twice. Once with a Springfield and once with..."

Bill nodded, "The M-1 Garand."

On the way back to Bill's house they talked about the M-1 Garand. Both of them had trained on it. Bill had carried it in combat throughout the Pacific war. It was a great rifle, shot a .30-06 bullet semi-automatically with the ammunition carried in an eight round clip. You could easily fire all eight rounds in 10 seconds. The drawback of the M-1 was that it ejected the empty shell straight up and back making it impossible to place a scope directly on top of the barrel. A scope for the M-1 was developed that mounted on the left side. They were not easily obtainable and you needed training to get good at it.

As they came into Bill's drive they could hear the phone ringing in his house. It kept ringing as they walked in to the kitchen. Frank went ahead of Bill, ducked inside and answered the phone. When Bill came in Frank held out the receiver. He had a grim look on his face and handed it to him.

He took the receiver and heard the voice of the Patrol Day Watch Commander, "Slim? Glad I caught both of you. Agent Dowd has gone missing. Have either of you seen him?"

Bill was only half listening, expecting to hear about Aggie, "What? No. What do you mean gone missing?"

The Day Watch Commander repeated himself, "Have you seen FBI Agent Dowd? Has he come to see you in the last two days?"

"What? No. Isn't this the FBI's job? I mean Christ on a cross how do they expect to find anybody if they can't keep track of their own agents?"

"Simmer down Slim, and listen up. I'm glad you haven't seen him and I'm glad you and Frank are out there. Everybody knows you and Dowd butt heads."

"Oh, hell's bells Charlie. Maybe he got tired of this place and caught a train back east."

"There's something else. He was checked through to the 300 Area. That was two days ago. He never checked out. The FBI says that we were probably sloppy and he didn't get processed out. But damn it Slim, nobody's been sloppy since Nate. He's out here somewhere. Tell Frank he is back on shift, everybody is going to be on until we get this straightened out."

"What about me?"

"Stay home. Take your pills. You still have another week."

Chapter Fifteen

Bill sat on the floor; hands laced behind his head and slowly did a sit up. He could do four. The first time he tried he only got two inches off the ground before the pain in his back lanced down his neck to his waist. Now he could do four. He turned over and started to do pushups. If he favored his left side he could do twenty. He stood and began to do the slow movements his Sensei had taught him in Japan. He remembered the small frowning man saying to him in broken English, "Slow to flow, long time before fast." Now he was very slow, moving, flexing, and finding the places where his muscles stretched against his wounds, old and new. His knee; where the ricochet from a Nambu machine gun clipped his kneecap, the right ankle he had broken falling off a horse when he was twelve, and now the deep purple red channel across his back.

He stopped, started again, remembered again his teacher, "No think! No head spin! Think, no flow!"

The phone rang. "We found him." It was Frank, talking low. "North side of the 300 Area. Not far from the B-pile. Between there and fabrication. It's bad. He was in a drum, would'a been buried if the stack hadn't been checked."

Later that day Bill was in the office. The patrol shirt scraped across his back and his head was throbbing slightly. He was not on the schedule but everyone ignored that. The relief watch commander had moved out front and Bill got his office back. Special Agent Parker called, "Heard you were back. Come on over, things have changed. It's now a task force and you are on it."

The FBI office was crowded. More agents had come in from Seattle and Portland. The new ones were sweating in the heat, not used to it. A conference room had been cleared and a map of the plant was tacked to one wall. The 100, 200 and 300 Areas were outlined in red. One of the permanent agents was at the front detailing what everyone was supposed to do and how it was to be handled. Another man, clearly not FBI, was asking a question.

"This isn't going to interfere with production is it? We are already on a tight schedule and if additional checks are run or areas shut down we will be falling behind.

All the agents in the room glared at the man. Another FBI man Bill recognized as Mel Jamison put on his best flat FBI tone and said to the man, "Those are legitimate concerns but we will not compromise an investigation, period."

The other man, who Bill now recognized as a managing supervisor from GE, didn't stop, "But with the new checks you said you'd set up at both K and Purex, shift change alone will take an extra hour, that's almost 35 hours a week of lost production."

Jamison's tone frosted over, "We are talking about matters of the highest national security. Please remember that you are here as a courtesy. Now are there other questions."

Bill, seated in the back, was content to watch the show. Of the 12 agents, three patrol members and two or three others

Bill could not identify, no one asked any more questions. Finally Agent Parker raised his hand, "Commander Bill Rosen has joined us, maybe he has a few comments he would like to make."

All eyes turned to Bill. The FBI agents' expressions ranged from detached to actively hostile. Jennings looked interested, the way you were interested in a suspect. Bill said, "I, uh, don't have anything at the moment. What type of weapon was used?"

There was a moment of silence. Jamison said, "Looks like a piece of rebar. His head was struck from behind and slightly to the right." Silence.

Bill shifted on his seat, "Where was he found again?" His shirt was tugging on his back.

The room was silent. "Agent Dowd was placed in a containment drum." Jamison, a man in his mid-thirties with close cropped black hair neatly parted, had lowered his head and was staring at Bill. He could see his blue eyes, they never wavered from his own.

"You said he was found by someone checking the drums. How?"

"How what?"

Bill wanted a smoke. He was getting a headache from sitting and the pain in his back was growing from an itch to an acid etched sharpness. "How and I guess by who was the drum found?"

There was grumbling from some of the other agents. Jamison picked up a file, shuffled through it, read, "Safety technician, Wayne Taylor, visually inspected drums before loading for trench burial, noticed one with an unlocked lid and proceeded to lock the lid when he noted an unusual smell, lifted the lid and discovered the body of Agent Dowd. That clear enough for you Rosen?"

"Not really. I'm just wondering. I mean the body or the barrel had to be moved, right? Unless he was killed right there."

"That hasn't been established, but so what?" Jamison dropped the file on the table.

"Well okay, still, why not seal the drum? I mean if the drum would have been buried he would never have shown up. All the killer would've had to do is use a drum wrench to seal the top."

"Maybe he couldn't find one." Jamison had backed off his attitude and seemed more interested.

"Maybe, but they are usually laying around or hanging on hooks close to where they stack and load drums."

"You think it means anything?"

"Think about it. Either Agent Dowd was lured there or taken there post mortem and put in the drum. It wouldn't take long. The top goes on, it's placed for disposal, but the killer doesn't take the few minutes to find the wrench and seal the top."

The room had stayed quiet, but the hostility seemed to be gone. Jamison picked up the file and took out a series of photos. He studied them and looked at Bill, "I still don't see, wait, you can see a latch space or something."

"I assume no prints were found, but here's the thing, maybe the killer knew enough to know a buried waste drum would be the perfect place to hide a body but not enough to know that unless it was sealed properly someone would check it." Bill stood and placed his back to the wall, giving himself some relief. "But it also had to be someone with a badge and enough clearance to go where he needed to go."

Jamison looked at the file, looked around the room and said, "Well, does this square with everyone else? Parker? You have the longest time here, does this sound right?"

Agent Parker cleared his throat, "Yeah, I didn't put it together, but yeah, that makes sense."

Jamison nodded at Bill, "Thanks Commander Rosen, this is the kind of cooperation we need. You all have your assignments. Dismissed."

Parker came over to Bill, "You don't look so hot, but thanks, this is why we need you."

Bill was standing, his back finally in a semi comfortable position. "Glad to help, is there anything else that is not being shared with the whole task force?"

Parker signaled for Bill to follow him to his office, and closed the door. "A couple of things, not a big deal, just curious."

Bill remained standing, the act of sitting made the stitches in his back feel like he had caught his zipper in his pubic hair. "Who was the agent in charge, anyway?"

"Guy from Portland, Mel Jamison. Good man, one of the best around, this thing has gotten big."

"It wasn't big when it was just a patrolman and some ref chemist?"

Parker was sorting papers on his desk, stopped, "Jesus Bill, that's not what I meant. You know the way the Bureau gets when an agent goes down. This thing was already big, now it's huge."

"Yeah I know, just something about getting shot makes me cranky."

"Okay, here is what I got. Dowd and Jennings had worked together for six months but Dowd maintained several confidential informants that Jennings did not know the identity of. That's unusual but not so much for Dowd. He was secretive, hinted at contacts in D.C. But maintained good files."

"So you got his files on his CI's?"

Parker leaned back, his chair creaking, "You sure you don't want to sit? You're making me nervous."

"I'm fine. Let me guess, they're missing."

"Not missing, just incomplete." He referred to a file he had open. "Dowd had several open cases that he had been allowed some discretion. He also had his own way of coding his files."

"So his mickey mouse chickenshit lives on."

"Watch it Bill. He was a good agent."

"I'm sure he was a great humanitarian. But as an agent he was a useless ass kisser and all around prick. So don't give me that good agent crap. What about Jennings? From what I've seen he has something on the ball, what's he say?"

"He was surprised we couldn't find anything. He said Dowd was pretty close about his individual cases. I don't know, he said he might have something on one of them, he's not sure of the name, might'a, could'a, should'a." Parker waived his hand in frustration.

"What's his story anyway? You said he's been here six months, but I didn't recognize him when he showed up in Nate's apartment."

"He's only been at Hanford for about a month. He skipped through a couple of times but he worked out of the

Seattle office. Before that D.C. He and Dowd have worked a couple of cases, low level stuff. You're right, Jennings is sharp."

"Okay, how about Aggie? And me for that matter." Bill started to reach across his chest for a cigarette, felt a sharp pain in his back and left them.

"You're not going to like it. It was brought up before you came in."

"Just let me have it for Christ sake."

"Not considered part of the ongoing investigations." Parker had stopped shuffling papers, held Bill's gaze.

"Why the hell not?" Bill finally sat on the edge of the chair.

"After the Bureau got cross ways with the Sheriff and the federal judge in the case, they decided to set it aside." He held up his hands, "Just for now. Everyone thinks it's linked. We figure that catching the killer in these two will tie up your case. We have all your information, Aggie has been cleared and is under protection. This way we concentrate on what we control and hope it falls into place."

"If Dowd hadn't been trying to screw me with this thing Aggie and I would be walking around fine and Dowd would be above ground." Bill got up and placed his hat on his head, "I'm going to the hospital and then home." He stood, felt the stitches stretch, "Parker, thanks, really, but watch your ass, this thing is not over and I worry about you."

"Me, why?"

"Didn't you hear your boys in there? You've been around the longest and know the most about this place. Lately that's been a recipe for getting shot."

He made his way across the lot and got into his truck for the short ride to the hospital. The cab was hot from sitting in the sun and he was careful not to rest his back against the seat. All the way over he kept thinking about Dowd, a miserable little man who was just looking for the big score that would make his career. He had found it and it had caved in his head.

The hospital was cool and quiet. This was reinforced with the rumbling of the large swamp coolers and a large sign that said, "Quiet please," above the desk of the reception nurse. Bill went to the nurse and asked about Aggie's condition. The nurse looked up at him over her glasses, paused and said, "Sign in Commander Rosen, visitation is strictly limited."

Having met many of her kind, no nonsense middle aged women in complete control of their jobs, he simply smiled and did as he was told.

Bill walked down the hall and into Aggie's room. It felt like a quiet cool space with the curtains drawn. A fan oscillated in the corner, stirring the air and dissipating a lingering smell of disinfectant. The oxygen tent was gone, but the ugly tube still ran from her chest to a collection bottle hanging off the side of the bed. The bed was cranked up slightly and she was propped on a couple of pillows. She had some color back, and her eyes fluttered and opened. She smiled and his gut unclenched. "Hey Bill," she said in a whispery voice, "How are you doing?"

"I'm jake, but you look a quart low." He put on a smile that was mostly real.

"Don't," She shook her head, "Don't make me laugh, please,"

"Cause it only hurts when you laugh, or breathe or do any other damn thing, I know." He then told her a long tale about cracking a rib while trying to save a calf from spring rains on the north end of Rattlesnake Mountain before the war. How he had to ride in the back of Johnny Buck's fruit truck all the way to Pasco. Then the Sisters at Our Lady of Lourdes put his arm in a sling and taped his ribs and told him he should not have bothered to come all that way. By the end Aggie had her hand to her mouth and was saying, "Stop for crying out loud, you'll kill me!"

A nurse came by, looked in and frowned, "Please keep your voices down."

"She's right," Aggie said, shifting slightly, "but you are the best medicine I've had." She lifted her hand off the sheet and took his. "Thanks for saving my life. Everybody told me what you did."

"Come on sister, I probably got you into this mess."

She frowned, "I don't think so. Nate..." She shook her head. "Any word? Everybody here is pretty mum on what's going on."

He looked out the window at a man walking behind a lawn mower, the putt putt putt of its engine coming through the closed window. "Nothing definite yet, don't worry, everybody is on it. I got to go. You rest and I'll check in later."

Soon he was back home with the quiet of the long afternoon. The air was clear and still, the heat rising off the sagebrush and sand. He threw a couple of eggs in a pan to boil, stripped off his uniform and changed into a pair of dungarees. Shirtless, he sat on his back porch, sipping a coke, careful to keep his back from touching anything. The heat soaked into his skin, warming and relaxing the muscles running down his spine. His eyes followed the view across the river, looking for the spot. He could just barely see the place where the shooter hid. He found it, thought to himself that it was quite a shot.

Chapter Sixteen

The phone ringing brought him out of sleep. Not really sleep, just the dozy semi-consciousness that he managed with his back stitched and itchy. He had been dreaming, or thought he had, where he was back in the Pacific War in the green dappled jungle. Mortar shells were coming down, but when they landed they went ring, ring, ring. He was in his own sweat soaked bed, looking around and hearing the phone. He stumbled out of bed and answered the phone.

It was Frank, working graveyard. "Commander Rosen? I shouldn't be calling you this time of night."

"What? What is it Frank? Spit it out. Is it Aggie?"

"Huh? No. Commander Rosen, you remember you assigned Swede to keep going through all the badge files to see if there were any close matches? Anything out of Two West?"

"Yeah, last he said was that everybody cleared. Everybody was at their job site and had signed in and out at the proper times." Bill stretched the cord of the phone over to the kitchen table. He sat and lit a cigarette. Took a drag, and put it out.

"Right. That's true. But Nate was a rover that night he was killed. He also checked in at Purex and then looped back to Two West."

"The chemist, or whatever, Ososkie, was at Purex, right?"

"Right, well it seems there was this other guy, let's see, Hank, or Henry that had been written up in connection with something. Wait, here it is, there had been a complaint by Ososkie for a safety violation against the supervisor, Henry Wilson. Investigating Officer Nate Bourbeau."

"Henry, Hank. Frank, you got his file in front of you. Wilson, the Supervisor?"

"Just a sec, yeah. Why?"

"What's in it?"

"Not much. Been here since '47. Huh. That's odd. Says his degree is from the University of Frankfurt. Name doesn't sound like he's a Kraut."

"Sure it does. It's just his name isn't Wilson. I'm on my way in. Call Agent Parker. Ron Parker. He's in the phone book. Call him at home and tell him to meet us at the Jadwin Barricade in an hour."

"Are you sure? The Feds will want this done by the book."

"Fuck the book. I'll swing by and meet you there."

He dressed in a hurry and felt the scab tear in his back. He could feel the heat in the channel down the stitches. He grabbed his hat and gun belt and headed for the door. The drive to the Jadwin Barricade was quick, like the night of the shooting. The night dark and moonless, the town quiet. The barricade was lit up as usual, the ten foot tall barb wire fence stretched to either side of it, dividing the project from the rest of the world. Frank was there, as was agent Parker. Agent Parker had just stepped out of the guard shack and walked to the back of his sedan, parked on the side of the road. Frank and Bill joined him as he opened the trunk.

"I called it in. I told them I was taking charge and that the Patrol was cooperating."

"That's not..."

"Can it, Bill. I just bought us a couple of hours. After that every federal agent from here to Portland will be crawling all over this place. The good news is it will take them that long to get up to speed. Just to be clear, this is your show for the next two hours, after that you have to back off."

"I'm not stopping after two hours. You know I won't stop 'til this is over."

"Then you better finish it quick."

Bill turned to Frank, "Is Wilson on tonight?"

Parker spoke up, "I checked. He came through at 11:00. He should be at Purex." He opened the trunk of the FBI sedan. Inside was a 12 gauge riot gun, a Thompson sub-machine gun and a scoped Remington rifle. "Think this will be enough?"

"You boys don't travel light. Frank, you okay with all this?"

Frank took the shotgun out of the trunk, racked open the slide, and filled his pockets with shells. "Ready."

Parker drove. The twin beams of the headlights pierced the darkness of the desert night. They drove with the windows down, the smell off the day heated pavement mixed with sage washed through the car. Parker, eyes steady on the road, "Walk me through it. We have enough to sweat this guy, but I want to hear how you put it all together."

Bill, sitting forward in the front seat, "There's still a piece or two that don't fit." He shifted, seeing a coyote on the side of the road, eyes luminous in the headlights, "Nate meets Wilson at work or at a bar. They spend time bullshiting each other, have some drinks, I don't know. Maybe they are short of money, looking for a score. They decide to brace the chemist, Ososkie, blackmail him or threaten to have him deported. That either works or it doesn't. They get in a row over it and Wilson pulls a gun. He shoots Nate at the edge of the pond and then after work pops by the chemist's house, gets him out to the shelter belt and shoots him there. Wipes the gun and leaves it hoping the whole thing looks like murder suicide."

Bill fell silent and Parker gave it a minute. "Where does Dowd come in?"

"Maybe he knew Wilson was a Kraut. Maybe he finally put two and two together. He wanted the score for himself so he confronts Wilson. He tries to bring him in alone and gets his head caved in."

"It's against Agency policy to make an arrest, especially on a secure government facility by yourself." Parker said, his voice rising.

"Easy. I know you don't like to hear it but Dowd was a glory hound. I could see him doing it."

"What about you and Aggie?"

"That's sketchier. Aggie was tied in to Nate. A loose end to be taken care of. My place in West Richland is isolated. Maybe he heard about Aggie and me from Nate."

"Could be. Not hard to get to the other side of the river from your place. Still, sounds thin."

"And there's Silky. She could have put Wilson and Nate together at Tiny's. So Wilson kills her to tie up a loose end."

Parker thought about it. You could see him working the angles. They turned onto the road leading to the Purex building. They stopped at the guard shack. Bill leaned out the window, "Hey Whitey, you got the call?"

"You bet Commander." He looked down at his clipboard. "Supervisor Wilson is in the building. What's up? I got another call from the FBI saying they will be here and not to let anyone leave."

"We'll let you know when we can. Who's on the desk inside?"

"Randow. You want me to call him?"

"Nope. Thanks Whitey."

They pulled into the sandy lot. As they got out Bill took the lead. "I go in first, Parker you're with me. Frank, hang back just a little."

They went through the door of the concrete 'canyon' of the Purex building. There was a guard desk and small office to one side. The looming interior was at least five stories tall, with gantries and cranes capable of moving the enriched uranium through the process of dissolving it in acid baths, a step in the concentration and extraction of plutonium. Purification and extraction, purex. In the background and all around them, workers in white cotton coveralls, some with hoods and masks, went about their tasks. At the desk a short patrol officer looked up from a stack of reports. He half rose but Bill waived him down.

"No need to get up. Is Supervisor Wilson on shift tonight?"

The officer looked through the papers on his desk and came up with a badge roster. "Yep. He's on the second tier. You want me to call him down?"

"No, we'll go find him. Is he in a hot area?"

"He shouldn't be. He should be doing log reports on the last run. Half way down take the stairs to the second level, there is an office at the top of the stairs.

Rosen and Parker headed toward the stairs. Bill turned to Parker, "Stay behind me. A patrol uniform is not out of place here, but with your suit you stick out."

The open metal stairs rattled as they made their way to the second tier. Open catwalks from the top of the stairs were suspended over open concrete pits containing solutions for dissolving the enriched uranium and separating it from the weapons grade plutonium. At the far end a glass paneled room looked over a gantry and crane assembly. Just off the side of the stairs there was an office with the door standing open. The light was on, a man sat behind the desk, beefy with a blond brushcut. He looked up as Bill came through the door.

"Henry Wilson?" Bill said as Parker came in and stood next him.

Wilson regarded them, relaxed, "Yeah. What? Somebody not sign in?"

"Something like that. Stand up. Slow." Bill motioned, "turn around, hands on top of your head."

"Fellas, there's got to be a mistake." He rose and placed his hands on his head, smiling.

Bill reached for his cuffs. Agent Parker had moved to one side of the office to give Bill room. At that moment Wilson pivoted and slammed his fist into Bill's chest knocking him back into Agent Parker. He was out the door and down the stairs before Bill and Parker could untangle themselves.

Bill was first up, drew his gun and started out after the fleeing Wilson. Wilson was at the foot of the stairs and running full out for the door. Bill was at least 20 feet behind him as he reached the bottom of the stairs and started for the door at a dead run. The officer on the door was facing away and had just turned and stood. He drew his service revolver and pointed it at the running man. Bill eased up thinking it was over when Wilson drew a small automatic and fired three times, the pop, pop, pop loud even against the sounds of the machinery in the building. The officer, Randow went down, clutching his chest.

Bill cursed under his breath, stopped and fired, his shot going wide. As he turned Wilson crouched and fired at Bill now using the officer's desk for cover. He leapt for the door and covered the distance in two steps. He was gone out the door and a moment later Bill heard the boom of the 12 gauge. The door swung open and Frank stuck his head in, "Commander Rosen? Agent Parker? You all right?"

Bill was crouched over the wounded officer. One of the white suited workers had gotten a first aid kit and was running toward them. Others were coming. Given the speed of what had happened and the background noise, many continued with their work. The wounded officer sat up, clutching his shoulder, "Dammit that stings. Sumbitch fired before I could even warn him."

Bill gently pushed him back down, "Easy Marv. You hold tight."

The worker with the first aid kit popped it open and began cutting expertly cutting away the officers uniform jacket. He looked at Bill, "I was a Navy Corpsman, I can handle this."

Agent Parker had moved past Bill and out the door. When Bill caught up he was talking to Frank, had his hand on his shoulder. They were both looking down at the still form of Wilson. He lay on is back with his arms outstretched, his chest a bloody mess where the buckshot had hit him.

Frank was talking fast, "Commander Rosen, I was just telling Agent Parker, I heard shots and then he came out the door so fast. He raised his gun, I saw it clearly." He stopped, looking between the two older men.

"You did good Frank, he took a piece out of Randow. You didn't have a choice."

"I never..."

"I know. Agent Parker, you have a problem with any of this?"

"No. He was faster than we thought. Looks like he was getting ready to make a move when we came in. Should have expected that."

Bill took the shotgun from Frank and laid it in the back seat of the sedan. "Let's go call this in. We'll be here most of the night getting statements."

Chapter Seventeen

Once again the hot sun of August was coming up as Bill drove back to his place. He carefully stripped off his uniform and stood under the tepid shower, the water sluicing down his head and front, letting some of it drip down his back and the wound channel. He couldn't see it but knew that the stitches had pulled, and blood had spotted his shirt when he had taken it off. He felt a warm dull throb from his injury, realized he needed to see the Doc again, that he was at risk for infection.

The FBI was keeping a lid on everything. There was no record of Wilson beyond what was in his personnel file, a bare bones jacket that looked as phony as a three dollar bill. But now the FBI had their reputation on the line, plus a few bodies, including an agent, so they would dig down deep. Bill turned off the shower. Dripping, he stepped out, wrapped a towel around his waist, briefly thought about going to bed and went to the kitchen to make coffee instead. He popped a penicillin pill, the bitter taste lingering in his mouth. He poured himself a cup, and went out his back door, looking at the small pane of glass that shattered when the first bullet had come through. He sat outside, the sun still low in the east, coming in under the porch and warming and drying his skin. He turned and let it warm his back, the wound drying in the morning sun. Heal up and hide over he thought, one of his father's favorite expressions. He looked at the shattered pane in the door again. From this angle he could see where it had chipped out the floor of living room. He moved over to see the line of sight through the door. The chip in the floor was offset from right to left. Something about the shot bothered him. No gun had been found, but it was certainly an M-1 Garand. The casings confirmed the caliber. The two quick shots had to be from a semi-auto rifle. There were thousands of Garands around, having been sold off after the war. He kept thinking about the scope, off-set to the left, remembered being on the firing range trying to snug it into his right shoulder and center his eye behind the scope. He did okay in his qualifications, but never got the hang of it.

Abruptly Bill got up and went to his phone. He called Frank's number. It rang twice before Frank picked up. "I'll be by in 20 minutes. There are some things we have to go over."

"Uh, Commander, I am supposed to be officially off for a week while the shooting is investigated. Everybody was pretty clear about that."

"Goddammit Frank. I'm coming by in 20 minutes. Now get shaved, put on your uniform and be ready when I come by. That's a goddamn order."

Frank came out of his house when Bill pulled up. He could see Frank's wife behind him, saying something and Frank making placating motions with his hands. As Frank walked to Bill's truck, his wife could be seen behind the screen door, arms folded, staring at Bill.

As they pulled away Frank, looking pale but clean cut as always, removed his hat and placed it with his gun belt next to him on the seat. "Commander Rosen, I don't think we should..."

"Let me guess, you came home last night, told your wife everything was fine and then sat up thinking about pulling the trigger on Wilson, right?"

"Sure, I guess."

"First man you ever killed?

Frank winced, "I never, no. I mean yes."

"So you ran it through your mind a thousand times, did a thousand what ifs, beat yourself up about how it should have played out, right?"

"Yeah sure, I guess."

"Right, then, that's over. Sitting around on your ass in your boxers for a week is not going to do you any more good."

They headed straight east on Van Giesen toward the river and turned left on a shady side street. Frank said, "Aren't we going to headquarters?"

"We need to get Parker and sort this out."

Agent Parker let them into the neat frame house. The neighborhood was beginning to wake up. Two boys on bikes with fishing poles pedaled toward the river. They sat at the dining room table, files spread out across it. Parker's pregnant wife Sue got them coffee. Bill nodded and Frank looked confused. Parker said, "I half expected you to come by. It doesn't quite add up does it?"

"On the contrary." Bill said, "It's too neat. All wrapped up with a bow. What do you have here, official files?"

"Yes, all cleared with the task force director. He gave me the files, told me to take the day off, stay home and write my report. What are you looking for?"

"You got pictures of the crime scene with Dowd?"

The file contained several typewritten pages plus photos. There was a black and white 8 x 10 photo of Dowd in the 55 gallon drum, curled up looking like he might be asleep except for the bloody crease in his short hair over his right ear. Blood had flowed down and soaked his shirt and pants, making them look black in the photo. Bill set them aside.

"What about Ososkie? Did you all do a final report on his shooting?"

Parker drew another file from the table. "It's here. Not much new. We confirmed that the bullet and gun match the Bourbeau shooting. It's a nine millimeter Walther by the way. Williams had a half empty box of nine millimeter pistol rounds in his apartment."

Bill looked up from the file, "You boys moved fast on that. Anything else."

"No. the place was pretty neat. There was a hunting type knife that might be a match for the Pasco murder. We are now going to treat that as related."

"So Silky might get some justice after all."

"It will be treated as related. With an agent's death involved, the full weight of the resources of the Bureau will be behind that investigation."

Frank, who had been sitting quietly finally said, "So this guy Williams did the four murders, Nate, Ososkie, Agent Dowd and Silky, and shot you and Aggie?"

Parker, turning back to the files, "Looks that way."

"No," said Bill. The room was silent. He rubbed his eyes, trying to push out some of the grit. Outside the day was fast heating up. Across the street children were shrieking as they ran through sprinklers. "Did Agent Jennings work the case last night?"

Parker thought a moment, "No. He was off."

"Good. Then he will be fresh. He's in today, right?"

"Everybody is."

Bill stood. "Let's get him and make another trip to where Dowd was killed and then swing back to 200 West. You think you can handle that Frank?"

Frank, his face reddened slightly, "Of course."

An hour later they were on the road in an FBI sedan. Parker and Jennings were in the front, with Bill and Frank in the back. The windows were down with the wind coming in to try to cool the riders. It made talking difficult but Jennings, arm over the seat spoke to Frank and Bill, "I'm glad you asked me along. You've been a big help in this investigation. I want to apologize for my partner earlier."

Bill, sitting up straight trying not to let his back bother him said, "Forget it. Dowd was who he was. Doesn't change the fact he was killed in the line of duty. We owe him."

They pulled into the large lot where the storage barrels were stacked waiting burial. The uniform light green barrels were stacked three high and ten deep. Empties were on the right. Filled barrels on the left were placed in a row five deep, waiting loading and transportation to the burial site. A section on the end was cordoned off with sawhorses and a rope. A sign was tacked to piece of plywood, *FBI Do Not Cross*. They made their way over to the site. Parker had the file open. "Pictures and good sketches. The tracks and tire marks are indicated here and here. Huh."

Bill, scanning the area turned, "What?"

"It's just. Look. The sand is soft. After he was found we went over the lot looking for tire marks but only came up with the set from Dowd's car, or at least another FBI sedan. In fact, there is only one set other than the skip loader used to haul the barrels." He flipped back a couple of pages.

Jennings looked over Parker's shoulder at the file, "So how did Dowd get out here? With the killer? And then the killer drives away and parks Dowd's sedan back in front of the FBI office? We checked his car and it doesn't look like it was moved."

Bill bent over to get a better look at the tracks. "What do you mean?"

"He usually parks it in the same spot. You know, he's, was, real picky about that. Wanted it in the shade and so on."

Frank had been quiet while the three men talked. Finally he asked, "Why kill Dowd? Killing an agent is the worst sort of trouble."

Bill stood, "Loose ends Frank, loose ends."

Frank wouldn't let it go. "What do you mean loose ends? Dowd was just one agent. Agent Jennings would have taken over."

Jennings was pointing his service revolver at them. He motioned with his gun for the three of them to stand together. "How'd you figure it out Bill?"

"I didn't. Not really. Wilson was left handed, right? Nate and Silky, at least from the reports were probably killed by someone left handed. But not Dowd. He was clocked from behind by someone right handed. You own a Girand, Jennings, with a scope? What's your play Jennings, why Aggie and why Dowd?"

Jennings stood silent, the gun trained on Bill, mouth set in a tight line. The sun was over the side of the stack of barrels, heating up the area. Finally he said, "I had been running Wilson for years, brought him out of Germany at the end of the war. Fucking Krauts. Supposed to be somebody big in the rocket program, but was just a Nazi party hack that worked in one of Speer's facilities. That was after we had scrubbed his record. He found Nate on his own. Those two were made for each other. Couple of two bit toughs always looking for an angle. The Feds were going to cut Wilson loose or send him back to Germany to face a war crimes trial. So what does he decide to do? Put the squeeze on some poor ref for traveling money. And Nate, always looking for an easy buck went along."

Parker, recovering his shock, "Bullshit. There was nothing in his files."

Jennings, the gun never wavering, "Parker, don't you get it? There are bigger players on the field now. The FBI is just a junior partner. You get the information we hand you and nothing more. Now drop your weapons and get in the fucking trunk."

The three men climbed into the trunk. Jennings, like he had done this before, stood back, covering all three, not taking any chances. Piled in on each other, road dust and the smell of grease in the stuffy darkness, they heard Jennings walk around and get in. The car started and moved off.

The car stopped after twenty minutes. Bill had ticked it off on his watch, the radium dial being the only illumination in the cramped trunk. They heard Jennings get out. This may be it, thought Bill. Instead he heard Jennings walk to the back and then the hiss of a tire, then around to the other three. They could feel the car settle slowly on its rims. In the desert quiet, they heard Jennings walk off and then a car start. The car drove away.

"Frank. Push against the back seat."

"I can't. Wait." They could hear the twang of seat cushions. Frank kicked again and the back seat of the sedan popped forward letting in light. By the time they all scrambled out, Jennings was gone. They stood blinking in the desert light, Rattlesnake rising up to the west and the Yakima winding in the distance to the south. Bill started walking down the slope headed toward the river. The other two looked at each other and then followed. Parker caught up first, "You saw the radio, right?"

"Busted," Bill said. His hat was gone and blood made a series of growing dots down his back.

"Where we headed?" Parker's cuffs starting to pick up burrs from the cheat grass.

"My place. We are not far and the river should only be knee deep."

"Good we can call and get a manhunt started."

"You do that. Seal the area and hope he hasn't made it past the Vantage Barricade. My thinking is he wouldn't have left us alive if he thought he couldn't make it out of here."

They trudged through the soft sand and sagebrush and down the bank toward the river. From where they were they could see Bill's house on the far bank. "You think this is how he got him out here?" Parker said to Bill.

"Wait. You think Jennings brought Agent Dowd out here and got the drop on him?" Frank said.

"Yeah. Makes sense. Maybe Jennings told him he had an idea or break in the case. Dowd's an eager beaver and would want to be in on it. Has him meet him out here. Takes him out to the waste pit and loads him into a barrel. Comes back out and takes his car and leaves us in the trunk."

"I still don't get it. Why are we alive? Why didn't he shoot us at the waste pit?"

"Who the hell knows? Maybe he figured we'd roast in the trunk. Maybe one dead agent was enough. My question to Parker is just who the hell was this guy? If he wasn't FBI then who was he? He didn't sound like a Red. He some kind of spy or what?"

Bill stopped and looked at Parker. Frank stopped and looked between the two. Parker started walking toward the river, "I'm out here at Hanford, I don't play politics. I rarely go to Seattle, but I hear things from people coming through. You may not know it but this is a place to do a tour if you want to move up. This is the big league. But lately," he shook his head, "It's getting beyond us, the sandbox is getting crowded. I don't know, but Jennings is some new creature out of D.C. Maybe the Pentagon, or maybe the CIA, who knows? But this place is made for him. Nobody talks and there are too many places to get rid of the bodies."

They made it across the Yakima and up the slope to Bill's house. Parker immediately called in a report and began mobilizing a search. A patrol car came out with the watch commander and took a statement from Bill and Frank. Both were told to have no further involvement in the case.

Jennings drove south out of Prosser. He had ducked a State Patrol roadblock at the last minute. He had parked on a side street and gone into a diner. He had waited. He thought he might try and bluff his way through but gave up the idea. He stopped at a Signal gas station, filled up and got a map. It showed a way through the hills to the south. If he could make it to

Biggs Junction, he could head west to Portland.

The late afternoon sun slanted across the long stretch of road. This long high ridge of hills sloped gently down to the Columbia River that could be seen far off in the distance. Jennings could see a farmer up ahead, his truck angled almost across the road, hood up, with him bent over the motor. Jennings slowed, hoping to ease around him, not wanting to risk the soft loamy shoulders. He stuck his head out the window, "Hey old timer, can I make it around you?"

Bill Rosen stood and turned, .45 leveled at Jennings, "Not this time Jennings."

Jennings hit the accelerator just as Bill shot him twice through the windshield. Bill dove out of the way as Jennings' car clipped the front of Bill's truck and bumped out into the stubble field of harvested winter wheat and stopped. Bill walked over, carefully looked inside. There were two holes in the windshield, one in the seat next to Jennings and one in his throat, just above the Adam's apple. A .38 was on the seat next to him.

Three weeks later he gave a copy of his report to Agent Parker. The official report of the inquest had already been forwarded to Washington. No mention was ever made of Agent Jennings again. Agent Dowd was hailed as a hero who cracked a murder case perpetrated by a foreign national at one of the nation's secret weapons facilities and died in the line of duty. Bill and Frank were commended for assisting Agent Dowd in his investigation.

"Do you think your report made it back to D.C.?"

"Doubt it. Maybe a paragraph or two. Anyway Doris made three copies. I gave one to the inquest, you get one and I'll keep the last one, in case my memory gets fuzzy."

"How's the back?"

Hurts like all get out. Doc said it's my fault, now it'll take longer to heal." He shrugged and then winced.

They were in Parker's office. Things had settled down after the inquest. The taskforce was disbanded, agents were reshuffled and everyone had signed papers pursuant to the National Secrets Act. Officially, Agent Dowd tracked down the killer of Nate Bourbeau and Ososkie and then just as he was about to apprehend the suspect he was killed. On Dowd's information the Hanford Patrol tried to arrest the suspect who was then shot as he tried to flee. Bill and Aggie's shooting was treated as unrelated and ruled a probable hunting accident. Silky's murder was left open.

"You never did say how you knew Jennings would be on that road." Bill always liked that about Parker, knew he could not let a detail like that go.

"Just a hunch. Nate went to Portland when he wanted to tie one on. Jennings probably knew that. I figured if he went west he would have a hard time getting past Prosser. Like I say, just a hunch."

Two months later Bill stood on the platform of the Pasco train station. It was a beautiful October morning, blue sky and a light breeze. Aggie wore a sun dress and straw hat. Bill had her suitcase.

"I'm gonna miss you kid."

"Me too. I'll write, but you probably won't. Come down to Los Alamos and see me. It's your kind of country." She looked down, around, anywhere but at him. The conductor called all aboard.

21486455R00118

Made in the USA
Charleston, SC
20 August 2013